the

GIRL

who

KEPT

WINTER

———

GIAO CHI

Table of Contents

CHAPTER 1

It Began With A Kiss

The long-awaited wedding of the town magistrate's dear son had become a funeral.

A sumptuous wedding feast had been prepared; the town was bright and beautiful beneath the colorful flags and resplendent flowers that had been used as decorations. A splendid dress had been carried to the bride's home. Vinh Phuc, the magistrate's son, was about to marry Dong Tu, the eldest daughter of the Luu family. This meant the most well-reputed dojo in the district would firmly be under the magistrate's control—and that the magistrate would finally be freed from all doubt about whether the Luu family, who had always appeared to run a well-respected dojo, was actually connected to a secret, criminal underworld: the Whispered World.

Luu Dong Tu was one of the most beautiful girls in the region, and a skilled martial artist on top of that, but that wasn't why the magistrate's spoiled son wanted her. Vinh

Phuc and Dong Tu had met by chance, and after receiving a sudden (but well-deserved) slap from Dong Tu, he had decided that he would have her as his wife, whatever the cost...if only so that he could force this unruly girl to bring him warm towels and wash his feet every day.

But that was not to be: for on the day of the wedding, Dong Tu died. Well and truly. Cold. Stiff. Dead.

The bride's family had obviously been trying to conceal something: they had stopped allowing the bridegroom's family to see her about a week before. Only when the magistrate made a fuss did they confess that Dong Tu had gone to guard a delivery being sent to the neighboring district, and that she would not return until closer to the wedding day.

Believing Dong Tu's father had lied to help his daughter flee the arranged marriage, the magistrate seized the family's property: the Luu dojo was surrounded by muscled henchmen for five days, the soldiers waiting impatiently for the family to give them a reason to strike. Under the pretense of preventing an uprising against the government, they would kill everyone, if given the chance. The magistrate would not have himself be made into a fool.

The shipment Dong Tu had escorted arrived safely, and the recipient confirmed that Dong Tu and the Luu guards had begun the journey home, assuring the magistrate that she had left in a hurry so she could make it home in time for the wedding. But five days later, there was no sign of the delivery team. The transport package had arrived, but the team had disappeared.

The magistrate's soldiers combed through all the neighboring villages, but came back empty-handed. It was as though they had evaporated into thin air.

Dong Tu's father swore on his life that his daughter would return before the wedding, and resolutely went on with the wedding preparations as if nothing had happened. And, miraculously enough, on the morning of the wedding, the ten guards sent with the delivery returned with Dong Tu still among them.

They could not hide their sickly, sallow skin, and several members vomited upon arrival, but neither they nor Dong Tu—who, though none of them had suffered any serious injury, was covered in dried blood—offered any explanation. Instead she quietly washed the blood from her body, put on her wedding dress and made up her face, and prepared herself.

The magistrate's council finally released the order to surround the Luu dojo, and the marriage was set to proceed as planned.

Just as the ceremony was about to start, Dong Tu said she was feeling lightheaded and needed a sip of tea. With that one sip, her face blanched, and she swayed, her beautiful gown fluttering around her; she hit the floor before anyone could catch her, and no matter how hard the family and guests tried to revive her, she would not wake.

Dong Tu's already sickly pale face had drained of all color by the time the physician arrived. Her lips had faded to a chilling gray, her breathing had stopped, and he could feel no pulse.

"The bride is dead!" he announced. "Death by poison."

Panic swept the room, guests dropping their cups or pushing them away, terrified that they would be next.

"Everyone, please!" the physician called over the ruckus. "It looks as though she was poisoned a few days ago." Vinh Phuc rushed forward and felt the cooling of Dong Tu's motionless body with his own hands; once he realized it wasn't some trick, he furiously demanded the punishment of the whole dojo. His bride had clearly committed suicide!

As Vinh Phuc went on furiously berating anyone in earshot, dark flakes, like blackened ash, began to fall from the ceiling. The flakes collected on Dong Tu's gown, and people leaned in to look, reaching out to touch them, to determine what on earth they were—and found the substance to be snow.

The guests looked up in confusion to see a man in black sitting calmly on the crossbeam. Even sitting, he appeared to be tall and strong, and he was dressed in layers of black clothing, covered with a black coat sewn through with many small, vertical metal tubes that looked to be armoring. In his black-gloved hands he held a metal staff. Perhaps his face might have been attractive, had it not been hidden by a blackened silver mask that showed only his eyes, and he watched the wedding party below, meeting their puzzled gazes with a cold, emotionless glare.

He didn't even flinch when a large scorpion slowly emerged from his coat and crawled across his shoulder, its tiny steps flicking those same snowflakes from his coat to float down upon guests looking up.

Snowflakes as black as obsidian.

No one had seen him enter. He did not speak, nor did he make any aggressive movement. For all anyone knew, he could have been there from the very beginning, just watching. Yet somehow, they all knew his appearance, his very presence there, was an omen of death.

Fear struck the guests again, that brief moment of calm turning once more into panic and disarray. The mysterious man glided gracefully to the ground amidst the madness. He considered the corpse, which had already begun to stiffen, turned, and strolled toward the door without another glance.

Both the magistrate's group and the Luu family unsheathed their swords in preparation for a fight, but before they could make a move, one of the guards who had arrived with Dong Tu shouted:

"Don't! Don't touch him! You'll die!"

Both clans stopped and stared at the stranger intently. Although this mysterious visitor was not equipped with a sword, within his outfit glinted the silver sheen of scales. The closer they looked, the more they could make out the forms or limbs of creatures, all wriggling and writhing; large black spiders could just be seen swaying within the shadowy darkness of his coat.

The whole room went silent; the guests parted like water to create a path as he left the building. As he passed, the only sound that could be heard was snakes hissing, and a communal shiver made its way through the guests. The air around him was freezing, surrounding his body with a faint, hazy cloud of steam as icy air met warm, and he left a trail of glittering black snowflakes in his wake.

Once the other man was gone, the same guard exclaimed, "That man is...he is...he was with the mutants in the forest. He was the one who killed Dong Tu!"

The physician cried out in shock and recoiled from Dong Tu's body as an inky black snowflake formed on her neck.

Duong Kien Minh—another martial arts master, and Vinh Phuc's teacher—recognized the mark.

"I know this mark," he said, panic turning him breathless. "People say there is only one man in this world who leaves a mark like that—a ruthless killer. He can kill hundreds of people just by flicking his hand, and he leaves behind the same mark on each dead body. He is the only person capable of using this poison. That man is definitely—"

———

Five days earlier, however, no one had expected such a tragedy at the wedding. And five days earlier, Dong Tu had still been very much alive.

"The hunchback can *fight?*"

Shock shot through Dong Tu like lightning. While she was lost in thought, silently lamenting her upcoming wedding, an elderly hunchbacked man, his deformed child, and his poor wife had appeared and begged the protective escort for food. Their pitiful appearance had prodded at her already heavy heart, and the party had stopped to give them what little they could spare.

Dong Tu had thought the man was old and frail, but then, without warning, he reached out and grabbed a fellow guard, swinging him easily above his head like a sack of straw. The hump on the man's back was like a turtle's shell, as hard as steel, and as a fight broke out between he and the guards and Dong Tu jumped into the fray, she saw that he used it as a shield.

At first Dong Tu assumed they must be bandits, but she quickly realized the hunchback was far too skilled—skilled enough to use a single pair of simple bronze bells to beat all ten members of their armed escort.

7

Even the deformed child, scaly-faced and lizard-like in appearance, was able to hit targets with a precision that should have required many more years of training than possible at his age. His nails were filed into sharp claws, and after each blow, he flicked out his tongue to lap up the blood.

The woman accompanying the miscreants did not bother to participate in the fight. She only stood there, lazily waving the fan in her hand as though she were attending a second-rate field match and expressing mild disappointment when Dong Tu's blows missed. She watched, yawning occasionally, as the two flashy strangers defeated the ten Luu guards.

Her escort group was beaten and bruised by the time they reached the middle of the wood. Only Dong Tu could stand up straight—because, curiously, every time one of the disfigured masters went to strike her, the woman had screamed out, "Ease up, watch out for her face!"

So while Dong Tu knew she was beaten, like a mouse being played with by a cat, the mutants never hit her hard enough to do any visible damage. Eventually it was her exhaustion that got the best of her, and she sank to the ground while the two strange masters laughed and mocked her.

"Who are you?" she demanded. "We are on our way back home—there is no more gold or silver to steal! So if you're going to kill me, kill me." Perhaps, deep down, a part of her had wanted to meet mountain bandits...for if she were killed in the middle of the woods, she wouldn't have to marry Vinh Phuc, and her family would be spared the consequences of the magistrate believing they had helped her escape.

"I am not a thief!" the woman snapped. "I don't enjoy killing." She huffed to the others, offended, "This girl doesn't even know who we are! Does she live under a rock?"

"If she had known, she wouldn't have played with us for this long," the hunchback chuckled. He pulled his shirt up to wipe the sweat off his face, cheerfully wiped his bells clean until they shone again, and then squinted at Dong Tu. "The girl is pretty good. She'd be going places in a few years, if she kept it up."

"What a shame," the reptilian man lamented. "But Switch wants her look today. Besides, I'm bored with her current face."

It was then that Dong Tu realized who the three strangers must be. The showy woman was Switch, the Skinwalker—which meant the other two had to be Leatherback and Anole. They were three of the eighteen infamous wandering mutants, collectively known as the Monstrous Eighteen.

It was said that the Monstrous Eighteen were strange in appearance, wielded extraordinary martial arts abilities, and moved in secret, so no one knew their true whereabouts. Some were good, some evil, but all were incredibly dangerous.

Dong Tu had heard the stories, but had never thought she'd meet even one of them. Now she was faced with three.

Switch approached Dong Tu and inspected her face.

"Not bad...but this face is so *homely*. It doesn't match my style." She scratched at her own cheeks; wherever she touched, her skin peeled off like dry plaster, one eye drooping as though it had melted.

Switch had been born without a face, Dong Tu recalled. She abducted people and used her *chi*—her innate power— to change her appearance, stealing the faces of those she had kidnapped. She must have wanted to test Dong Tu's power, and now she wanted to steal her face, too.

Dong Tu looked closely at Switch's current face, guessing that it would soon morph into her own. Switch always chose a beautiful girl, and her current face wasn't so bad; but it was old, and had started to crack and peel away. If she'd had a choice, that wasn't the kind of face Dong Tu would have chosen for herself.

She took a deep breath. Now more than ever she felt like a drowning person clinging to a thin branch.

"Beautiful lady, do you want my face?" she offered sweetly. "You can have it. Even better, you can be me and marry into a wealthy family and share in their immense riches. It will be a luxurious life."

"Why? Are you being forced to marry someone? I can have gold and jewelry whenever I want; I have no need to marry."

Crap. Dong Tu took a second to recover, then tried another avenue.

"But I'm already about to be married off. If you walk around with my face, you'll be arrested! Can't you just pretend to be me until the wedding is over?"

The three mutants laughed again. They weren't concerned by the thought of the military chasing them, and they didn't care about Dong Tu's situation. But when Switch started dipping into her power to change her face, Anole stopped her.

"Wait a minute. This girl is fun! Let's bring her home tonight, we need a drinking buddy!"

The hunchback cheerfully agreed.

And so, that night, Dong Tu found herself huddled with the three mutants in a tattered hut nearby, drinking while they caroused and babbled drunken nonsense. The ten bruised and injured guards had been locked up in the stables behind the hut, and Dong Tu wanted to help them, but there was nothing she could do while at the mercy of her freakish captors.

Leatherback was not as old as he'd claimed to be, she learned as the night went on. He did have a hunched back, and when he took off his shirt, the skin there was rough and had the texture of a tortoise shell. He wasn't attractive (to put it kindly), but he had gentle eyes—though when he drank, he spat out endless insults about the other eccentrics. He soon began telling the other deformed masters' stories: how they had each been rejected by their people and had banded together for companionship. They were brilliant at martial arts, but the eighteen of them were only seen as misshapen freaks, cast out by society.

Dong Tu relaxed in their company as they drank, and eventually she even began to see them as human beneath their scarred exteriors.

Anole was a child born out of wedlock, the son of an official. The official's main wife had tried to kill him, an unwanted bastard; but the family's servants took pity on him, taking him away and hiding him in a bamboo basket. As he grew, the tight weave confined him, disfiguring his limbs and muscles. His deformed hands and feet made his movements clumsy, and as he grew older, his permanently disfigured body turned grotesque. But despite all his defects and the danger to his life, he'd yearned to discover his true identity.

Switch used to be a faceless child, a genderless outcast. The face she wore was beautiful, but the face she'd been born with had terrified those around her. As the hunchback told her story, her hand clenched around her cup, and she drained cup after cup trying to ignore his recounting of her ugly past. When she reached the point of being truly sloshed, she relaxed enough to let her voice deepen to an almost manly pitch, giving credence to the hunchback's story.

Then Dong Tu was asked about her own story. Because Anole was eager to learn more about his noble identity, when he heard the word *magistrate* mentioned, he began asking her about Vinh Phuc.

Dong Tu said, "Vinh Phuc is pampered and spoiled, and that's all you need to know."

Dong Tu hadn't known who Vinh Phuc was when they met; just that she had only ever seen him surrounded by servants. Whenever he said anything, they all agreed with him, bobbing their heads vigorously. The two of them had tried to buy the same horse at the market, and Vinh Phuc had "accidentally" touched Dong Tu where he should not have—which had resulted in him receiving the fateful "slap from heaven."

By the time Dong Tu finished her own story, the three mutants were asleep.

Her first instinct was to take advantage of their drunken slumber and flee; but something stopped her. Despite their bizarre appearances, these three mutants seemed more pitiful than scary...and right now, she herself was pitiful. She felt a strange sense of sympathy for them, and so, rather than escape, she pulled a blanket up to cover the hunchback. She got up to pour herself a cup of water—

And at that moment the door was kicked open, revealing a new man. Black clothing covered every inch of his skin from head to toe, and a silver-and-black mask concealed his face. An unseasonable chill washed over the room as he entered, and a few odd, black flakes swirled through the cold air.

"Who is this?" he demanded when he laid eyes on Dong Tu. "Get her out!"

"That is my new face. Don't touch it," Switch responded, rousing from her sleep.

There was something about the man that struck visible fear and discomfort into the mutants: wherever he went, Anole and Switch would shrink away.

The man in black leaned in and peered more closely at Dong Tu.

"Too ugly," he said. "Since when do you like this kind of face?"

Anger flared to life in Dong Tu, hot and fast; too drunk to control her impulses, she reached out and jerked down his mask, tossing it to the ground.

"You think *I'm* ugly? You're the one hiding your face! How pretty could *you* be?"

She immediately regretted it.

While she had expected someone disfigured and hideous, this new stranger was, in fact, surprisingly handsome. His bone structure was chiseled and strong, his eyes bright and his lashes thick. Dong Tu wasn't able to recover her composure in time, and she gaped at him for what felt like an eternity. The man frowned and hurriedly covered his face with his hand.

"Your face—you don't have to hide it," Dong Tu murmured with a shake of her head, her face red and her eyes wide. After meeting these three deformed masters and hearing tales all her life about the Monstrous Eighteen, facing such a handsome so-called *mutant* was completely unexpected.

"Wrong!" Anole called with a smirk, but despite the smirk he chewed on his claws, clearly jealous to see that Dong Tu was blushing.

Switch shook her head, snapping out, "This idiot!"

The last to wake, Leatherback managed to open his eyes, the lids heavy with drink. It took a moment for the scene to register, but when it did he hurriedly shouted, "Dong Tu, stay away from him!"

But he was too late. At that moment, Dong Tu and the man in black both bent over to pick up the mask at the same time; and while her hand brushed against his black glove, her lips lightly grazed the man's cheek in passing.

Like a fleeting kiss.

Like a breeze...

They had just met for the first time, but when her lips touched his cheek, she felt as if she'd been shocked. Except... something was wrong. This couldn't be the kind of heart-pounding thrill she'd read about, not when the initial jolt kept *burning*.

Dong Tu went limp, her body numbing, and she collapsed helplessly to the ground.

All the other eccentric masters stared in shock

"You two just kissed!" They shrieked in tandem, for all the world like preteen girls.

"My new face is ruined!" Switch cried, dramatically bereft.

Anole crawled closer and watched Dong Tu, eyes wide with disbelief.

"You just touched...you touched him!"

Dong Tu couldn't understand what was going on, and she couldn't speak to ask. A stinging poison was rapidly making its way from her lips to every part of her body. It was like an electric current, making her painfully aware of the location of every single one of her nerves, her body twitching until, bit by bit, she was paralyzed.

Everything seemed to fade. The pain, the room. The only thing Dong Tu was aware of was the distant-sounding voices of the mutants.

"She doesn't know of Obsidian?"

"Did you two kiss?"

"It wasn't a kiss."

"Your first kiss?"

"It wasn't a kiss!"

Switch leaned in close to Dong Tu.

"You were wrong. He doesn't wear a mask to hide his face—he wears one so that no one can touch it! That man is Obsidian—the King of Poison. Even masters like us dare not touch his skin."

"Was that your first kiss?" Switch asked the man in black again as she straightened.

"It wasn't a kiss!"

"Oh, so sweet! Obsidian's first kiss!"

"It wasn't a kiss!"

Anole and Switch continued to squabble, ignoring the girl rapidly losing consciousness on the floor beside them.

Obsidian squatted beside her, holding a pill to her numb lips. "I don't have a true antidote," he said. "I'm sorry."

Dong Tu swallowed it with what little energy she had left, knowing she had no time to consider the consequences when her breathing was becoming shallower and shallower. After a beat, she began to feel less numb, and her breathing eased.

"If you can't save it, then what is the point of holding on to it for a few more hours?" Switch looked the saddest of any of them. "You owe me a face, Obsidian."

CHAPTER 2

It Continued With A Kiss

Leatherback was upset: Switch only cared about Dong Tu's poisoning because she could no longer steal her face. She couldn't care less about the girl slowly losing her life next to her.

"She's so cute...so sad," the hunchback sighed.

But they all knew there was nothing they could do. There was no antidote to the poison that laced Obsidian's skin.

"...So how should we handle her and the people in the stable?" Anole finally asked.

"Who's in the stable?"

The three mutants led Obsidian to the stable and pointed out the ten Luu guards who lay, bruised and dirty, amidst the straw.

Obsidian stiffened as he looked over the prisoners, his hands curling into tight fists. So Switch and Anole considered this place and these humans their playground, discarding their trophies in the dust and muck? He struck the two of them with his gloved palm in two swift hits, knocking Anole and Switch back with such force that they landed almost six feet away.

The Luu family's guards were already injured, and now, caught in the crossfire between three eccentric masters, their injuries were about to be much worse.

By the time Anole, Switch, Leatherback and Obsidian all returned to the main house, clearly worse for the wear, Dong Tu was nowhere to be seen.

The girl should have died within a few minutes. Thanks to the Poison Restraint pill, she had been given the chance to cling onto life for a few hours more, but it couldn't have healed her. How had she managed to heave herself away?

"Go find her. Get her back."

"That was your first kiss."

"It was not a kiss!"

They continued to quarrel animatedly. The deformed masters were bored: wandering from place to place, outcast by society, was less interesting than it sounded. They'd been lacking a thrill in their lives for many years—and someone "kissing" Obsidian was *monumental*.

Meanwhile, Dong Tu had managed to reach the creek. Her wedding would be held in four days: if she and the agents did not return by the wedding day, the magistrate would have plenty of reasons to ruin her whole family. She had wanted nothing more than to escape her wedding...but in the face of inevitable, horrible death, all she wanted was to return home.

Dong Tu pulled herself up and continued to heave her leaden body through the woods, forcing one foot ahead of the other, one at a time. Not long after she left the creek, she began to catch glimpses of a warm light through the dark pines. A campfire? She fought down the hope in her heart. People?

As she got closer she saw them for what they were: a group of mountain marauders, assaulting an elderly woman.

Normally, these marauders would not have stood a chance against Dong Tu, but the poison had wrecked her body. Keeping herself upright was a struggle, let alone swinging a sword. But, as she watched the mountain marauders kick the old woman and grab at her bag, Dong Tu could not hold down her rage. She lifted her sword with all her strength and shouted:

"Enough! If you are wise, you'll give the bag back to the lady!"

"That's her! The girl who keeps winter! I finally see her!" the elderly woman called excitedly.

As soon as the marauders saw the beautiful young woman, angry yet alone in the middle of the woods, they howled with delight and charged her.

Dong Tu held her sword tight. She intended to fight until her last breath.

But as it turned out, fighting was unnecessary—because at that moment Obsidian emerged from the trees.

He was not wearing his mask, revealing a tired frown that darkened his young face, but the moment he saw the marauders a murderous gleam appeared in his cold eyes.

"The girl and the old lady come with me."

The marauders fell into peals of laughter. The Monstrous Eighteen were not known to live in that area. The name Obsidian wasn't unfamiliar to them, but the *kid* before them gave them no pause; all they saw was an unarmed, bitter, and angry young man staring them all down. There was no way he could be the ruthless killer of legend.

The marauders aimed their spears, intending to teach him a lesson. But, within seconds, centipedes were crawling and writhing out from every crevice in the forest. Obsidian's long shadow cast triangles on the wet grass, from which snakes crawled and hissed, and black snow began to flood the air around them.

The marauders wasted no time and fled, screaming: there were powers at work here that they dared not face.

Once they were gone, Obsidian scowled at the old lady.

"The Stargazer should have known that there would be marauders, shouldn't she?"

The old lady chuckled and leaned down to pick up the bag the marauders had dropped, and while she and Obsidian were focused on each other, Dong Tu studied her more closely. Her wrinkled face showed no signs of distress from the attack: she was serene, content, as if being saved had been her plan all along. Her robe was bursting with color, and glittered dully as the low light of night glinted off the precious stones embroidered along its surface; and Dong Tu could finally see that the bag the marauders had tried to steal was also full of precious gems and pearls.

The old lady looked at Obsidian, eyes narrowed, and said: "Bold statement. Mind the arrow."

Turning to Dong Tu, her expression changed to one of concern.

"This young lady looks...sweet. A little *ordinary*, compared to what I expected. But that's okay." She put her hand on Dong Tu's shoulder and continued more gently. "You who keep winter, whatever you do tonight, you must think carefully. Just one move, and you could start a war that spans the whole world."

Dong Tu didn't understand what the old lady was saying. She was just a girl from an obscure dojo and an unknown family, not a person from the wandering eccentrics' Whispered World. And she was dying of poison! How could she do *anything* to turn everyone in the world against each other?

The lady explained nothing more. She merely awarded Dong Tu a mysterious smile, climbed onto her horse, and galloped away. The thundering hooves splattered dirt all over Obsidian's clothes.

"Nonsense. Get out of here, Fortune Cookies," he muttered.

The Stargazer—if it really had been her—was yet another of the Monstrous Eighteen. While she did not study martial arts, she had the divine ability to see into the future and read the past, so it was even more puzzling that she seemed to have tried to come here just to see Dong Tu's face.

Stir up a war...*what?*

When the old woman was gone, Dong Tu and Obsidian were left staring at each other in an awkward silence, Obsidian still brooding, Dong Tu exhausted.

He finally broke the silence. "The Poison Restraint...it will only keep you alive until dawn."

"Then please, give me the antidote."

"There is no antidote for this."

"So why did you come looking for me?" Dong Tu asked wearily, skeptically.

"The hunchback wanted you to take those ten men back to their dojo."

"Release them. They will go back by themselves." Another uncomfortable silence fell between them; Obsidian gave no reply. "...Is that really why you came after me?"

The man still did not answer.

Dong Tu's yearning for home returned, and, exhausted and rambling, she began to tell him her whole story, right from the start. Even as she stood on the threshold waiting for death. She spoke of how she wanted to go back, to let everyone know that she hadn't run away. How she couldn't let her family be punished needlessly.

Obsidian didn't reply, but he didn't stop her, either, and so Dong Tu continued to relay everything that had happened to her, avoiding eye contact by gazing up at the stars. She explained all about the arranged marriage, about her worries for her family. Eventually, a heavy thump jolted her back to the present, and she turned to see Obsidian flat on the ground, unconscious.

Obsidian, a formidable, almost legendary figure whom even the other extraordinary masters feared, had crumpled straight to the ground without explanation.

Dong Tu only had a few hours left, and now it seemed she would have to decide between leaving him there, or staying to see what had happened. She took a step closer and wrinkled her nose as she looked at him from a short ways away: his body was crawling with snakes and spiders again. Getting to him would be a nightmare.

And yet Dong Tu decided to stay.

"You have impeccable timing," she muttered to his limp form as she used a stick to flick the snakes and spiders away, and bent to brush away the thin layer of black snow that had gathered on his body.

Then she hesitated. Just barely brushing her lips against his skin had been a death sentence: how could she take care of this man without risking touching him again? But then, she was already dying. What was a little more poison?

Dong Tu opened up his coat first. When she found nothing visible she frowned resolutely, and—with a good deal of effort, given that Obsidian was nothing but dead weight—began to strip his robe off as well. His body was a canvas of scars: a big scar slashed across his chest, and his shoulders were crosshatched with what looked like scratches from fingernails.

"Scratches all over your shoulders...I wonder what kind of game you were playing, and with whom?" she muttered to herself. He was lethal to touch, and from what she'd heard, he was a powerful fighter—so how could anyone have gotten close enough to leave such marks on his body at all?

Not finding any injuries on his front, Dong Tu rolled Obsidian over and stopped: there was a deep, stinking arrow wound in his back, just above his shoulder blade. The arrow was still buried in his skin; most of the shaft had broken off, and what little was left protruded garishly from the festering wound.

Mind the arrow, the Stargazer had said. She'd been right.

The skin around the wound was coated in oozing, bloody infection, and without his clothing there to soak some of it in—and after being jarred in the fall—the wound began to bleed freely again. Dong Tu looked around for something that would help and saw his coat again: she pulled it to her, meaning to search for pockets, and her eyes widened when she realized that what she'd thought were metal pieces sewn into the coat as armoring were, in fact, little metal vials. Could one of them contain medicine? Could one of them be the antidote *she* needed?

She opened them all, smelling and examining the various powders that filled each; some of them had to be poisons, others antidotes, but if there was something in there that could help either of them, it wasn't any kind of medicine or herb she recognized. In the end she gave up and decided to use what little she had at hand to work on Obsidian. Setting her jaw resolutely, Dong Tu reached in with her fingers and started to work the arrowhead out of his body.

Blood began to pour from the wound, drenching her hands and smearing up her arms, streaking her face and mouth when she tried to wipe the sweat from her brow or brush a hair from in front of her face.

The arrowhead came free with a shocking spurt of blood that managed to hit Dong Tu straight in the face, as she'd leaned in closer in her determination. She hurriedly tore strips off her dress, spitting Obsidian's blood off to the side, and used the strips as rags to wipe up the mess and then as bandages to help stem the bleeding. His skin was surprisingly warm, and she realized that, beneath the coppery tang of blood on the air, he smelled pleasantly like herbs.

Exhausted, vaguely shellshocked, and coated in the man's blood, Dong Tu took a moment to breathe and look him over again. Now that she wasn't focused solely on removing the arrow and stopping the bleeding, she allowed herself to examine his back as well.

Her stomach dropped.

Somehow, in the midst of all that, she'd been so focused on his wound that she'd missed the massive, inky black spider tattooed across his back.

Or *was* it tattooed...? Dong Tu reached out, horrified and yet fascinated, and ran her fingertips along the image. The texture of his skin itself was strange, not at all like a normal, healed tattoo, almost as if the skin beneath were all scar tissue—but, more than that, the spider seemed to rise up out of his body like it was attempting to break through the skin. Its legs and body were all raised, and whatever lay beneath his skin there was not flesh. Whatever was beneath his skin was hard and unyielding.

"Who could have done this to you?" Dong Tu murmured.

Not far away, the Stargazer pulled her horse to a stop.

"She has chosen Obsidian. Our world will never again be as it was."

———

The sun slowly rose up from the east. Obsidian woke with it, aching and exhausted, and saw that his body was bandaged... in flowery fabric. He panicked for a moment, and then sighed: fortunately for him, Anole and Switch were not present. If they'd seen him covered with flowery bandages, he would never have heard the end of it.

Dong Tu was curled up like a sleeping kitten beside him, her clothes bloodied and in tatters, and he realized she was the only one who could have tended to his wounds the way they'd obviously been cared for.

Her face was lively in her slumber. He wondered what she was dreaming of.

As he studied her, Obsidian realized Dong Tu was far prettier than he'd given her credit for. Compared with the ethereal beauty of the faces that Switch often chose, she was nothing special; but compared to ordinary girls, Dong Tu was very pretty indeed. And there was something sweet about her, as she slept so soundly beside him, that made her seem even cuter.

Looking at Dong Tu, his gaze trailing over her round cheeks and beautiful mouth, Obsidian remembered the feeling of Dong Tu's lips against his cheek, however clumsy the moment may have been.

"Your first kiss!"

"It was not a kiss!"

Her lips had been soft, delicate. Warm.

For the first time in his life, Obsidian allowed himself to touch an outsider's skin with his bare hand. For the first time, he touched someone without any intention of killing them. For the first time, his fingers traced the curve of a girl's soft, silken mouth.

"It was not a kiss!"

Had it really been a kiss?

"If it was a kiss, it should have been on the lips, shouldn't it?" he asked aloud of no one.

Obsidian lowered himself back down and studied Dong Tu's face, her mouth, more closely.

"Why am I not dead?"

Dong Tu's eyes snapped open, the question uttered as though from a dream. She jumped when she saw Obsidian right in front of her, startled to find that he'd gently laid his finger over her lips.

Why was he so close?

"Well..." Obsidian cleared his throat. He knew why Dong Tu was still alive, but the information, the way to neutralize the poison on his skin, was too precious to reveal. If he revealed it, he would be endangering his own life.

"Because I gave you a pill. But it's only a temporary fix. You will live for just a few more days."

"You mean there really is no antidote?" Dong Tu pressed sadly, hoping that Obsidian would show her mercy. It seemed somehow sadder to him now, when the sweetness of her sleep hadn't been pushed from his mind yet.

"No. There isn't." Obsidian's tone was quiet, but final. He began pulling on his clothes to cover the flowery fabric bandaging his wound. When he finished dressing, he looked around with a steadily increasing sense of panic.

"Where is Greeny!?"

As it turned out, the creatures Dong Tu had flicked away from Obsidian's body the night before were his...pets. *Pets*. Venomous snakes, spiders, and scorpions. Greeny, Pretty, Scaley. All pets. And she had "lost" them while trying to save him.

Dong Tu wasn't sure it was really much of a loss.

Obsidian rushed to find them. Fortunately, he seemed to know exactly where the creatures would hide in the forest, using his bare hands to catch the scorpions and spiders, and within a moment he had found his countless pets. He even showed off a little: he touched his lips and whistled softly, and the snake, Greeny, slithered out as if from nowhere. He grinned like a child receiving a gift when his beloved snake returned to him, and, in a rare showing, dimples appeared in his cheeks.

He probably only has snakes for company, Dong Tu thought to herself. *If a normal person showed such a look and smile all the time, he would have countless friends.* She didn't understand who Obsidian was, but in the few hours she'd known him, he'd seemed perpetually lonely, cold and distant, as if his body and his soul were in two different places.

Despite the fact that she'd lost her fear of him long before, once she knew what was somehow hiding in his coat, Dong Tu kept her distance as they began the walk back to the Luu dojo—no matter how true Obsidian's assertion that his pets would never attack unless bidden might have been.

But Obsidian was indebted to Dong Tu. She had taken care of him when she didn't have to, even risking herself. He gave her four more pills, and told her they would hold her in this life through the wedding: there was no way to remove the toxins, but Dong Tu would definitely live long enough that the magistrate and his son would not seek their revenge on her family.

"If I have to marry Vinh Phuc, what's the difference between life or death anyway?" Dong Tu sighed. "Maybe being poisoned isn't such bad luck."

As they traveled, she began to remember the legends she had heard. Of a man whose fighting skill was virtually unknown because no one had ever fought him and lived to tell the tale; a man who had trained on his own body from a young age, until he and the poison had become one. His skin, flesh, blood, and sweat were all said to be toxic. She knew now that Obsidian carried thousands of different kinds of poison, and that he could kill people without ever getting close—and that not even the legendary King of Poison had an antidote to the toxin that laced his skin.

But Obsidian was not a ruthless killer. He didn't wear the mask and all his layers to menace or intimidate; he wore them to protect everyone else.

Which also meant no one knew he was actually young and handsome beneath the silvery mask and that cold glare, and that no girl had ever dared to kiss him.

Except for one...and now Dong Tu.

An unusual sense of guilt weighed on Obsidian as he thought about what had happened. He kept his distance while escorting her back, and watched her with narrowed, pondering eyes. What was he going to do with this girl?

The two said nothing to each other during the journey. But, every once in a while, their eyes would meet as they snuck glances at each other, and each time they both blushed and turned away.

Dong Tu knew the mountain and the surrounding forest well. She had often traveled back and forth while escorting her father's packages, paying little attention to the view. But this time the scenery was unusually beautiful. The shady road was dappled with golden sunshine that filtered down through the leaves. The breeze, gentle as butterfly wings, carried fluffy white dandelion heads on their mysterious journeys, and came laden with the scent of fresh grass, blooming flowers, and all the richness of nature. Small birds ran busily up and down the tree trunks, and the silhouettes of small creatures springing effortlessly between branches flickered and darted overhead. Even the gravel on the road seemed beautiful, the sharp fragments of deep brown, red, and slate blue twinkling where dewdrops and sunlight came together.

She didn't know if it was the poison, or if she was simply mesmerized by the scenery, but Dong Tu felt light, as if she could have floated away, and the time passed by in a daze.

———

Soon enough, the night fell and they took a break to build a fire to cook dinner. As Dong Tu was raking at the dry leaves, she looked up to see several figures in immaculately white clothing emerging from the darkness like gods stepping out of a painting. Their footfalls were so light it looked as if they were floating. As they drew closer, Dong Tu could see only one man, armed with a bow, and seven ethereal women with ribbons dangling from their clothes. They too wore masks, and simple, tight-fitting gloves.

The group froze, then immediately took battle-ready stances the moment they saw Obsidian; he stiffened, and once again was overtaken by that bone-chilling coldness, drawing his silver staff.

The others attacked from afar rather than charging in; it was obvious they'd fought Obsidian before. The archer was lightning-fast, and in just a few seconds he'd shot dozens of arrows from his bow while the seven women attacked, wielding their silk ribbons as lethal weapons. They covered their mouths, blocking the poison powder Obsidian threw, and whipped and twisted their silk ribbons around him. And then one of them gracefully kicked a pile of coal into the air.

All it took was one small spark. Tongues of flame shot up the ribbons twisted around Obsidian, and while he was momentarily dazzled by the sudden flames, the man in white raised his bow and aimed.

"Watch out!" Dong Tu shouted, and then one of the seven women whipped a silk ribbon around her ankles and jerked her feet out from beneath her.

At that moment, Anole, Leatherback, and Switch rushed out of the darkness and grabbed Obsidian's shoulders. All four disappeared, escaping back into the night, leaving Dong Tu with the white-clad archer and the seven women as they furiously put out the fire-wreathed silks. The archer came closer, helping Dong Tu back to her feet.

He took off his mask, revealing himself to be another handsome young man with a striking face. He looked innocent, almost angelic; the softness in his face, Dong Tu noticed, was strangely similar to how Obsidian had been when she'd caught him watching her. But this newcomer was confident, not skulking, full of a welcoming warmth— and Dong Tu got the distinct impression he knew exactly how handsome he was.

The women accompanying him also took off their masks, all in perfect synchronicity. All of them had soft white skin, and a freshness about them, like fairies from the watercolor paintings Dong Tu had sometimes seen in fancy houses.

"Because of this *little girl,* we've lost him again!" the woman who had whipped the silk ribbon at Dong Tu said bitterly.

Another young woman asked, "Sir, what should we do? The Elderess needs the Storm Pearl now!"

The white-shirted man raised his hand to silence the two women, and then he brushed his hand over Dong Tu's ash-covered cheeks.

"Little girl, are you okay?"

"I'm not a little girl," Dong Tu muttered.

The other girl—the beautiful but ferocious Iron Sky— interrupted again.

"Bach Duong, sir, what if this girl is his accomplice?"

So the white-shirted archer was named Bach Duong. Once again, he shushed the women, looking Dong Tu over

36

with concern. All it took was one glance at her face for him to know that she was a hair's breadth from death—and it was obvious to him that she was just an ordinary person, not a master warrior like them.

"I can give you something to help," Bach Duong assured her. He squeezed Dong Tu's mouth open from the sides and dropped in yet another pill. "This pill can restrain Obsidian's poison in your body. As long as you don't use your chi, the poison won't reactivate. Ever."

It was the first time someone had said that any antidote for Obsidian's poison existed. And whether she believed it or not, it was too late—because the pill had dissolved as soon as it had entered her mouth.

Bach Duong saw Dong Tu's disgruntlement, and he smiled and stroked her cheek. Dong Tu blushed and pushed his hand away, but the man still leaned down to kiss her cheek. All seven women gritted their teeth and looked away as Dong Tu gaped in shock, and Bach Duong chuckled softly.

"She's so innocent. Goodbye, little girl. The best of luck to you!" The archer bid his farewell and disappeared into the darkness as well. The seven young women turned and followed him, each of them managing to give Dong Tu either a jealous or sympathetic look on their way. Iron Sky stalked away as if she wanted to devour Dong Tu whole.

Once she was alone again, Dong Tu sat down, her face flushed.

"I'm...I'm not a little girl."

She was rightfully shaken by the encounter, and it took her a while to pull herself together; but after a while, Dong Tu realized she could no longer feel the dull ache of the poison still lingering in her body. It was almost as if the poison had vanished completely.

Bach Duong's kiss hadn't just surprised Dong Tu, it had also surprised the four eccentrics watching from in hiding—especially Obsidian. He, Anole, Leatherback, and Switch had hidden themselves in a nearby tree, watching the group below like hawks. Anole and Switch silently reveled in the moment, while Leatherback's face twisted into a mischievously knowing grin. All of them enjoyed the drama, until they noticed that between the way Obsidian was wrathfully grinding his teeth and the embers still burning across his clothing, he was fuming in more ways than one.

The three disfigured masters shared a look, hiding how thrilled they were by this development behind carefully crafted expressions of sympathy.

"Your rival kissed your lover!"

"She's not my lover."

"But she *was* your first kiss."

"It was not a kiss!"

Switch blinked slowly and taunted him: "Whether it was a real kiss or not, Bach Duong *did* kiss her!"

"She's a Bach girl now!" Anole added.

"Jealous?" Leatherback asked, and Obsidian glared at him.

"No!"

"You're smoking!" Anole teased.

"Just the sparks from that fire!" Obsidian clenched his jaw and pounded at the ash that still lingered on his shoulder. Then he jumped down from the tree and disappeared.

The three remaining wanderers looked at each other with impish glee. Nothing this amusing had happened in years.

CHAPTER 3

And a Problematic Kiss

Despite the initial excitement, Anole and Switch soon grew sick of the ten captured guards in the horse stable. At first it had been amusing to have the stiff, straight-faced men serve them their meals in the manner of high-class butlers, act out elaborate plays, and pose as targets for fruit-throwing competitions. The mutants had even forced them to dance. To their surprise, however, the thrill of watching a highly trained fighter click his heels together while trying not to trip over stray piles of straw did wear off eventually.

The guards of the Luu family were trained martial artists, and while they were solid enough to stand the mutants' wicked tricks, they were clumsy at important tasks—namely housework. This meant that Leatherback had to cook for thirteen mouths. By the third day, he felt as though he were running a daycare center, unwillingly taking care of the ten guards while the other mutants sat around and complained of their boredom. None of them wanted to take the responsibility for finding a place to dump ten corpses, so, without much need for discussion, they decided to kick the Luu guards out for good.

Thus, after many days of suffering, the guards were finally released. They ran as fast as they could, weaving between the forest's densely grown trees until, finally, they caught sight of Dong Tu.

Any relief they had felt melted away into dread.

Dong Tu stood with her back to them, and facing her was Obsidian, once again wrapped in his black coat. The two stared at each other, silent and motionless, but a dark intent seemed to radiate outwards from Obsidian like pain from a wound. His lip curled in a silent snarl and he struck; her body crumpled instantly to the ground. Without a word, he calmly slipped the mask over his face, turned, and walked away. The Luu guards drew back to let him pass, averting their eyes to avoid his icy gaze. The air froze around them as Obsidian walked by, leaving behind the telltale sprinkling of black snow.

When Obsidian was far enough away, they stumbled forward to help Dong Tu up. She fell back against a tree and coughed up black blood, her face pale and her pulse erratic. For a moment the guards watched in panic, until Dong Tu heaved herself upright and waved them away.

"It's okay...just sorting out an unpaid debt," she muttered. They waited for her to catch her breath, then resolutely headed off in the direction of the dojo. All of them were dotted with bruises and cuts, leaning on each other as they marched through the days and nights. They finally arrived at the dojo as the sun rose on the morning of the wedding.

The school was surrounded by the large, muscled henchmen of Vinh Phuc. The man himself pushed two of them aside as he strode in, cursing as he headed straight for Dong Tu with murder in his eyes, shouting about a runaway bride.

"I did not run away," Dong Tu denied firmly, meeting his gaze without blinking. "You can start the wedding as you planned."

At the sight of his bride's steely eyes, Vinh Phuc ordered his troops to withdraw from the dojo.

And so, just as planned, the wedding began. Drums, horns, and the melodies composed by the wheeling birds overhead filled the air, while flower lanterns drifted lazily upwards into the open sky. Dong Tu wore her intricately embroidered wedding dress patterned with white and gold flowers.

And, hours later, the colorful flowers were replaced with black ribbons, and the guests solemnly removed their jewelry, the extravagance inappropriate for an occasion of mourning.

Vinh Phuc, of course, refused to take the bride's corpse. A corpse could not bring him a warm towel to clean his feet.

Eventually, since Dong Tu and Vinh Phuc had not actually been married before she died, Dong Tu's body was given to her own family and kept at the Luu family's dojo.

The person who was hit hardest by Dong Tu's death—aside from her family—was Bao Thuong, who had been adopted by the Luu family at a young age. He'd been brought there to learn martial arts, growing up to be a martial arts master and hired guard at the dojo. Bao Thuong and Dong Tu had been raised together, practicing together since childhood, but his feelings towards her had long evolved past the protective instinct of an older brother. For years he had dreamed of her in a wedding dress, one remarkably similar to the one she had been wearing that day. But the groom had been all wrong.

Sure, the Luu family had two other daughters, Xuan Thu and Bao Yen. Xuan Thu was smart and bright, but only liked playing instruments, singing, and reciting poems. Bao Yen was too young. Dong Tu was the only one in his heart.

When he'd heard the news that Dong Tu was caught in an arranged marriage, Bao Thuong had taken his anger out by practicing his kicks and punches on random objects, knowing that there was nothing he could do that could stop it. And then Dong Tu died on her wedding day, and

Bao Thuong's heart was broken. He neither ate nor slept, spending every waking hour kneeling over her coffin.

Two days later found Bao Thuong still silently studying Dong Tu's pale, lifeless face in her coffin. He halfheartedly beat his fist against his chest, considering—not for the first time—whether he should die along with her. His throat, sore from two days of weeping and screaming, cracked in protest when he tried to shout, and he returned to kneeling and staring at the coffin in silence, unblinking.

Bao Thuong's behavior grew more erratic when the troublemakers came.

First it was Vinh Phuc. He was nowhere to be seen on the first night, but on the second, Vinh Phuc hid from his teacher and snuck out, along with four bodyguards and three of his maids. They'd come to see Dong Tu's face: he wanted to make sure that the Luu family had not fooled him.

When they arrived, Bao Thuong rushed at the four bodyguards, striking out recklessly with his fists to stop them from getting closer to the coffin. Eventually Dong Tu's sister, Xuan Thu—a girl who was normally gentle and polite—shouted Bao Thuong down and forced him to stop. She knew that Vinh Phuc's gang was looking for an excuse to take their anger out on someone, and the more Bao Thuong provoked them, the more reason they would have.

She stepped forward and said, "If you want to see Dong Tu, then come and take a look."

She heaved the lid of the coffin off for Vinh Phuc, unceremoniously revealing the corpse that had once been Dong Tu.

"Our sister was taken from us by poison, and her body was toxic. There were four people in our family who helped prepare her body, and they were all poisoned, too. But if you want to take her body, then so be it."

Taken aback by Xuan Thu's warning, Vinh Phuc did not come any closer than necessary, stopping when he was able to see Dong Tu lying stiff inside the coffin, her eyes closed and her face a ghastly, graying white. He ordered his people to keep back.

The fuss Vinh Phuc's appearance caused only made Bao Thuong's heart heavier. He grasped the corner of the coffin and cried out, "Dong Tu was plagued by trouble her whole life, and now, even once she has passed away, you still cannot let her rest?"

Bao Thuong's mourning once again sparked a wave of bitterness through Xuan Thu and Dong Tu's two elder brothers, Luu Tien and Luu Ky.

Just as Vinh Phuc and his people left, another group arrived. This time it was Bach Duong, along with his seven beautiful women, all dressed in white. Bach Duong moved slowly, encircled by women on all sides, and floated into the hall like prince charming. He came to the coffin, touched Dong Tu's cheek, and examined the mark on her neck.

"This menace, Obsidian, has no mercy even for the innocent. I gave her the cure and she healed, only to be struck by him again." He sighed, shaking his head.

"May I ask how you know my sister?" Xuan Thu asked, seeing that this group was much more well-mannered than the last. Bach Duong thought for a moment.

"A good friend," he answered vaguely. Deciding to question him no further, the family invited them to stay for the night; and soon, exhausted by the evening's events, the whole family went to get some rest. Only Bao Thuong remained, keeping vigil over Dong Tu's coffin.

Around midnight Xuan Thu awoke to bring some food for Bao Thuong—just as a third uninvited guest showed up.

Not fussy, aggressive, and disrespectful like the spoiled son of the magistrate, nor poetic and beautiful like Bach Duong and his women, this guest came alone. His step was quiet, save that each footfall brought with it the echo of scales slithering over leaves.

The doors creaked open with a rush of cold air and a flurry of black snowflakes that glittered in the moonlight like tiny slivers of obsidian, blowing out half the candles in the hall in a swift wave. The wind caught the white mourning curtain that shielded Dong Tu's coffin and lifted it, revealing everything that lay behind; a piece of fabric came free and drifted and swirled down onto the stranger's shoulder. He calmly pushed the curtain aside as he removed his mask.

47

Xuan Thu and Bao Thuong's eyes widened in recognition.

There were only three people in the hall. Xuan Thu hadn't been trained to fight; Bao Thuong was just an ordinary guard of the Luu dojo. But the guest who had just entered was an infamous member of the Monstrous Eighteen: Obsidian, the King of Poison.

More than that, he was the one who'd killed Dong Tu, whose body lay enclosed in the coffin at their feet.

A strange fog had accompanied Obsidian into the hall, one that seemed to move of its own accord, and soon the swirling mist engulfed the room. With their next breaths, Xuan Thu and Bao Thuong's muscles ceased to obey them: they could neither speak nor move. They could only watch and see what he would do next.

Obsidian's face betrayed no emotion at all as he took off his mask. He opened the coffin's lid and lightly touched Dong Tu, the mottled white of her skin making the black snowflake stand out even more clearly than before. He lifted the girl's body and sat it on the ground, propped up against the coffin. He examined the snowflake on her neck carefully, before tearing her shirt to reveal another snowflake mark on her chest.

As Obsidian handled the body, both Xuan Thu and Bao Thuong struggled to control their grief and anger. Seeing this abomination grope Dong Tu, Bao Thuong bit his lip so hard that blood began to trickle down his chin.

Obsidian pressed his fingers onto each point of the snowflake on Dong Tu's chest and neck. Where his fingers made contact, small needles slowly began to emerge from her skin. He collected the needles at a leisurely pace, seemingly unconcerned by the fact that Xuan Thu and Bao Thuong were both staring in forcibly silent desperation.

Xuan Thu was not as aggressive as Bao Thuong, nor was she capable of using her chi, so she kept silent and observed. She kept an eye out for any indecent behavior Obsidian might have toward the corpse, but was perplexed to spot none. On the contrary, Obsidian seemed to touch Dong Tu gently...as though he wanted to transmit his chi to her. His hand was pinkish, a more human hue than the rest of his body, and a ring of light glowed where it made contact with her skin.

An unbelievable thought occurred to Xuan Thu: Obsidian might have good intentions. Just as she was grappling with this idea, he pulled Dong Tu close to him, and tenderly blew a line of smoke across her lips.

Dong Tu did not stir, but Obsidian persisted; the smoke lingered and began to curl around her blank, lifeless face. Obsidian watched intently, his gaze gentle, holding her as though she might shatter if he gripped too tight—and after a beat the bone-white shade of her skin began to take on a rosy cast.

The scent of her skin stirred memories within Obsidian as Dong Tu lay on his chest: of her lips touching his cheek the night they first met, or the second day, when he'd woken up first and had watched her sleep. Once again Dong Tu looked like she was deeply asleep. Her eyes were closed, her face relaxed, her body softening in his arms from the stiffness brought on by death. Her lips were parted, just a breath away...and every time he blinked, his eyelashes lightly brushed against her cold cheeks.

He drank her presence in, forgetting the world around him, and the iciness of his demeanor began to melt back into that rare softness that had only been glimpsed at before.

That was why, while he was trying to transfer his internal chi into Dong Tu, *right* in the middle of the funeral hall, Xuan Thu and Bao Thuong were forced to watch helplessly as Obsidian closed the distance between himself and Dong Tu and kissed her. It was soft at first, his mouth tenderly brushing against her lower lip; then he became more daring and deepened the kiss. The heat of Obsidian's body melted the cold on Dong Tu's lips, and, as if she could feel his touch, her lips slowly began to move against his in return.

Obsidian jumped and went still, struck by the sudden, visceral reality of what exactly was happening. He didn't pull away even though he'd frozen, torn between finally letting himself have this contact and tearing himself away as he knew he should. And when he finally forced himself to pull away, he watched her face with somber eyes and a heavy sigh.

Bao Thuong and Xuan Thu were so astonished that their faces managed to betray their own absolute shock. Xuan Thu had, for a moment, allowed herself to believe that Obsidian might have had good intentions, and she was the most stricken of all to see how wrong she was. Seeing the mutant kiss her sister like that, slowly, tenderly, like they'd been lovers...that shining moment of hope that she might have seen some good in his handsome face vanished with a rush of cold horror. And still the two were trapped, watching helplessly as Obsidian cradled Dong Tu's body.

Not long after, Dong Tu's mother passed by and noticed that most of the candles were out, absent-mindedly entering the hall to relight them. She stopped when she saw the same black-clad figure from the wedding holding her daughter's body on the floor, faced by two people standing as stiff as statues; she recognized Bao Thuong—though his face was distorted, as if someone had ripped his heart from his chest— and shouted for help.

Obsidian jerked in surprise, and any softness in his eyes drained away as the whole of the Luu dojo came pouring into the hall. Even Bach Duong and the seven women came, bows drawn, arrows nocked and ready.

The attack on Obsidian was instant: they had to regain Dong Tu's body. But Obsidian didn't move: one of his hands remained flat on her chest, pouring healing chi into her body, and he fended off his attackers with the other. Bao Thuong charged in to slash at him the second he was released from his unnatural paralysis, but Obsidian blocked the blade with his hand. The metal blackened and seemed to wilt at his touch, and everyone looked on in disbelief as the blade splintered like a toothpick.

Even one-handed and distracted on the ground, Obsidian outmatched everyone from the dojo, proving the legends true: he really was one of the greatest masters in existence.

But Bach Duong and his seven beauties weren't ordinary people, either. They'd fought Obsidian many times, and after putting that arrow in his back, they were confident they had him. Yet as the women aimed their arrows at Obsidian, Bach Duong signaled them to wait: he'd finally realized what Obsidian was doing there on the floor.

The King of Poison was, in fact, trying to revive Dong Tu with his chi. If they wounded him now, she would die—permanently.

The two sides glared at each other, waiting, the atmosphere as tense as the seven drawn bowstrings. All eyes focused on Dong Tu, who remained motionless.

Suddenly the silence was split with a gasp as Dong Tu's eyes struggled to blink open, and her fingers shook as she tried to move.

That seemed to be enough for Bach Duong and his seven women: the women released their arrows the moment that gasp rent the air.

But Obsidian had not finished reviving Dong Tu.

He caught seven arrows in one sweeping motion. And, just as he lowered his hand, the sound of an eighth arrow being loosed cut coldly through the air.

Dong Tu blinked as she woke up. Her eyelashes were stuck together in the unnatural cold, and her body felt stiff, as though she had slowly been fossilized. One after another, warm drops, like fresh rain in the summer, ran down her cheek and pooled on her lips, leaving a slightly salty, metallic taste in her mouth.

Her vision cleared slowly, the world around her still distant, as if she were listening and looking through the muffling depths of water. The dark shape above her sharpened until she saw a figure clad in black, seemingly surrounded by a dark cloud; she blinked again, and she realized that black cloud was really the soft fall of a familiar dark, aberrant snow. She focused on his face and frowned as she recognized Obsidian, but something was wrong.

The young man's handsome face was twisted in a grimace, and a pained grunt made it through her haze like an echo. Dong Tu let her gaze travel lower and blinked in clouded, distant shock: an arrow had pierced straight through his throat.

The world around her seemed to fade away. She could see the candlelight reflecting in the vivid, almost entrancing red rivulets as blood rolled down his skin. She could see the growing gleam as the rivulets became a smooth stream of crimson. She could hear the echoing splash and patter of the blood as it rained over her, the way the sound changed as the blood began to pool.

But still Obsidian's hand stayed on her chest, and she felt his chi as it flowed into her very heart.

CHAPTER 4

Storm Power

"Saliva exchange...and face to face like that. *That* was a kiss!"

"Not worth taking an arrow in the throat. What a fool!" Anole said.

"It's romantic!" Switch argued. "If only someone would kiss me like that!"

"Maybe we shouldn't have kicked that guy out the door and forced him to chase her down the other night..."

As daggers were drawn, the hunchback chuckled, then replied rather bluntly.

"This Dong Tu girl...she's not too pretty, she can't fight as well as the rest of us, and her chi is weak...but just because she looks so young, kind-hearted, and stupid, like a puppy, everyone wants her."

The news had flown to the ears of the Monstrous Three faster than the arrow that had buried itself in Obsidian's neck.

Perhaps news traveled fast, or perhaps it was because the three were squatting on the roof, watching the whole thing from start to finish. From Obsidian's sudden kiss to his insistence on giving Dong Tu his chi, even when faced with flying arrows—the three on the roof had seen everything.

"That brat. Despite his appearance, Obsidian knows how to love." Anole couldn't wrap his head around the mess in front of him: Obsidian was normally so cold and distant.

"It's best to die in love. Love only lasts forever if the lovers die!" Switch snapped at Leatherback. When it came to love, Anole and the hunchback were not often able to argue with Switch. The truth was that those two had never had so much as a summer fling before. The two of them were the very embodiment of forever alone.

Switch, however, was different. It helped that she was able to swap her face with the most beautiful girls in the world. She always had men following her. Switch had loved and was loved a lot. Boys and girls. Tall and short. Loud and quiet. She knew the classic love story inside out. Yet something had happened that had led Switch to leave her turbulent love life behind her.

Switch, the Skinwalker, was a free spirit. The word "consequences" did not seem to feature in her vocabulary. So when she saw a beautiful girl, she would normally be wearing that girl's appearance within a few hours, with little thought of the owner. At one point in her life, she'd been trying on faces like other girls tried on dresses. If she didn't change it every day and night, a face could last for a few years. But there was nothing that could make Switch keep a face for more than a season.

The incident had happened in a rare moment of quiet, as Switch sat at the bank of a flowing river, watching the water swirling over the stones. She had looked across at the opposite bank, where a girl was humming to herself while washing clothes. Her face was so beautiful that Switch immediately rushed across the river to make it her own.

Wanting to show off her new look, she had entered the nearby town, where the girl had come from—only to discover that she was married. He was a gentle husband who pampered his wife with all his heart. Seeing this honest and beautiful man, Switch had pretended to be his wife, only to be able to spend more time with him. At first it was little more than a curious game...but she soon discovered that she loved him dearly.

The woman she was impersonating had known her husband since childhood. Their lives had unfolded like a lazily written romance novel: they had grown up and realized that the love of their life had been in front of them all along. They had even lived on the same street. Billions of people in the world; what were the odds? It was all rather convenient, Switch had thought. They were perfect for each other, their lives were perfect, and they were in the process of perfectly living happily ever after.

"At that time, I would have given up everything, just to live under that simple thatched roof like a normal person in a happy marriage," Switch recalled when she told her companions the tale.

"And then?" Anole and Leatherback leaned forward in anticipation.

"It was time to make a new face."

Within a few years, the face Switch was using began to age and crack. It was high time for her to find a replacement. However, how was she to put on a new face and still return as the wife he loved? This one would also be beautiful, but it wouldn't be the face of the husband's old wife.

"I nervously returned home, not sure how to explain," Switch recalled with distant eyes. She'd entered the house with her new face, claiming herself to be the wife's cousin, and told him a story of how his wife had died.

"I convinced him that his wife's dying wish was that she wanted me to take care of him on her behalf. So, since then, we have continued to stay there and live a happily married life. We love each other passionately!" Switch concluded.

Anole and Leatherback gaped at her.

"So...what's the matter?"

"The problem is," Switch began, with a hint of annoyance. These men didn't understand at all. "The problem is that there are no problems at all! I changed my face several more times...once I was his wife's cousin, another time I told him I was his wife's other relative, even said I was her confidante. I changed my face five—no, six times. The husband still lived happily. Every time he lost a wife, he loved his new wife just as much as the previous ones."

Anole and the hunchback still sat with blank looks on their faces.

"I mean, although there were many wives, with many different faces, the fact is that it's still just one person, me, Switch. I am the new wife and the ex-wives at the same time. So who am I jealous of? Seeing that my husband loved every wife the same as the old one, it's as though it doesn't matter who she is, as long as she is his wife. The new wife came to replace the old one, and the old one was forgotten! So, what is love? If you really love me, how can you love others so quickly, exactly the same and just as passionately?"

At that point Anole and Leatherback had finally begun to understand her suffering, even if they still didn't quite see how her logic was working.

Now, despite the reminder of Switch's love life, however tragic, their minds were quickly distracted by the love story currently facing them.

Dong Tu had known that she would wake up that night. But she hadn't expected to find her savior suddenly bleeding out, or to find herself sitting right in the middle of a fight between him and Bach Duong, someone else she hadn't expected to find in her home. On one side, Obsidian was bleeding profusely, his face hardened, his usual cold even colder. On the other side, the handsome and elegant Bach Duong also glared, this time determined to defeat the King of Poison.

That Obsidian was no ordinary fighter had been proven repeatedly even over the past few minutes: he had just defeated the Luu family with only one hand. It was even known that beyond the traditional arts, he had trained his body like an athlete to attain the ability to poison with only a touch, and that was impressive in itself. But few people knew that was not his only power.

There was another primal force living within him.

He had just been shot through the neck, and had poured enormous amounts of energy into Dong Tu. Anyone else who had been injured as he was would have been dead already. But, somehow, Obsidian still had the strength to break the arrow and fight back.

Even Anole, Switch and Leatherback, his three closest companions, were astonished by the amount of power he began to draw on. As he steeled himself, preparing for another attack, all three of them paled and exclaimed, *"The Storm Strike?!"*

The Storm Strike was a technique far more legendary than Obsidian.

"I thought that was only an exaggerated old story!" Leatherback exclaimed excitedly. "Only those who have swallowed the Storm Pearl, forged over the course of hundreds of years, can control it! The Storm Strike carries all the force of a hurricane—just one blast from the Storm Strike can smash the surrounding forest into wood pulp! I didn't know Obsidian bore such power inside his body! He must have the Pearl!"

Just as the hunchback finished speaking, the wind began to rush, and a cyclone rose up from Obsidian and twisted straight into the sky. The entire hall shook with thunderous rumbling, and black snowflakes whipped through the air like gathering crows. The whole dojo panicked, people flocking together like sheep, unable to see who they were clinging to through the icy storm. Bach Duong's bow was shattered by a gust of twisting wind.

Obsidian threw a warning glance in Dong Tu's direction, grimacing with the effort it took to control the storm, his teeth gritted in preparation for the upcoming strike.

"RUN!" The three eccentric masters on the rooftop screamed, and flew to find places to hide.

Bach Duong's team drew together in their own panic. The seven women formed a ring around Bach Duong, hoping to shield him from what came next—but no strike came.

After a tense few minutes the wind began to die down, the gale of snowflakes settling.

Obsidian was gone.

Was it because Dong Tu would have been harmed? Or was there any reason at all?

Bach Duong was frustrated at having lost Obsidian yet again, but he couldn't deny his relief. They all feared the wrath of that wind.

"That's the first time the Storm Strike has ever been witnessed. If the Whispered World knew Obsidian had the Pearl, he would never be able to rest," Leatherback said. "Either way, he seems to be seriously injured—both injured and hunted. This guy is dead."

Switch nodded.

"Wherever he goes, snowflakes fall. It's not exactly easy for him to hide."

"It's lucky that he didn't attack, or else Bach Duong's girls would have shattered into pieces!" Leatherback added.

Bach Duong heard what the hunchback said, and he resisted the urge to send an arrow through his throat, too: Dong Tu, finally fully cognizant, had made it clear to those around her that both Bach Duong and the three deformed masters were guests. Guests must respect the host and not fight in the school—or the owner will kick them out.

Bach Duong and the Monstrous Three growled at each other, but they kept themselves in check. A fight was definitely brewing, but it would have to wait for morning's light.

————

Bach Duong was an odd man. Odd in personality, but with a unique and charmingly beautiful appearance. His clothes and his hair could inspire joy in those who looked at him. As soon as the storm had dissolved, Bach Duong's clothes had shone once again, and his hair had returned to its perfectly groomed state. He'd even smelled delicious, as if he had just finished bathing—while the three wandering masters and the people from the dojo stood, bedraggled, in the wake of the storm.

He seemed to be a decent person, not the kind of man who started fights for fun. He'd used an antidote to save Dong Tu from Obsidian's toxins, after all. And the girls who followed him were also graceful and polite.

But Bach Duong had at least one glaring flaw: his penchant for kissing pretty girls unasked-for at the first encounter, like the first time he'd met Dong Tu in the woods. Now, as Dong Tu woke up, he approached her.

"It was the Soul Streak!"

The Soul Streak was a special type of toxin, one that could cause the appearance of death within the person it affected. That person could live again if a strong enough chi were passed through their body. It was rare, too—only the descendants of the Poison Legion were meant to know about it.

Bach Duong finished explaining, leaning closer to Dong Tu and giving her yet another wet kiss on the cheek.

"That was the trick. He helped you to fake your own death, and escape from your marriage!"

Dong Tu irritably wiped his saliva off her cheek. Bach Duong scratched his chin.

"While the Soul Streak is mysterious and potentially useful for faking one's death, the one who wields it must be extremely powerful, otherwise they risk their own life. I never would have guessed that Obsidian would spend such raw energy...just for a girl!"

Dong Tu knew that well. On her way back home, the day the Streak had been embedded, Obsidian had suddenly appeared in front of her.

"Bach Duong gave you that antidote. If you do not use your own chi, the poison will not break free. It won't kill you," he had said. "Thank you for helping me bandage my wound the other night. In return, I will help you escape from this wedding. And when you wake up, let it be even between us."

Once he'd finished his explanation of the Soul Streak, the Obsidian had sunk the needles into Dong Tu's chest.

The other guards had found her just after.

Dong Tu mulled over the memory. He'd been shot because he'd been trying to revive her, trying to even the score between them, but he'd only been hurt again in the process. The thought weighed on her.

The other man, Bach Duong...Dong Tu owed him a favor, but he had wounded the one for whom she held affection and gratitude. She turned to him.

"Who are you? How do you know so much about Obsidian?"

CHAPTER 5

Sunlight Power

Bach Duong snickered.

He was an attractive guy, and he knew it. Whenever he talked or laughed, he made a point to flash his gleaming, straight, white teeth. Occasionally, he would slowly blink his beautiful, lively eyes just to bat his long, thick eyelashes. He really was a rare kind of handsome. But even while looking at Bach Duong, Dong Tu couldn't stop herself from thinking about Obsidian.

Obsidian was not as conventionally good-looking as Bach Duong, but that was because he wasn't the kind of flashy, gaudy man who spent hours perfecting his look in front of the mirror. Rather, Obsidian seemed to be a person who was accustomed to solitude, speaking few words and avoiding the spotlight. Dong Tu had sometimes thought, as they'd journeyed through the woods, that Obsidian had feelings for her but didn't want to say it out loud. He didn't particularly seem like he interacted with women on a regular basis.

Meanwhile, on an average day, Bach Duong would have seven beautiful women accompanying him wherever he went. He had an impressive figure, and was used to assuming that every girl who met him would like him. He was always the first to make a move—on their behalf, he thought. It always seemed obvious to him that women wanted him, but dared not make the first move; he never considered that maybe some of them just weren't interested.

Therefore, after only a few sentences of conversation, Bach Duong would naturally get close and caress the girl's face. Or, if she was particularly pretty, he saw no wrong in briefly touching his lips to her cheek.

If it weren't for the fact that he'd saved her life by giving her the antidote, Dong Tu would have slapped him a good few times by now.

Xuan Thu was different. She may have had no proficiency in the martial arts, but Xuan Thu could read people like she had a manual. Bach Duong approached with a plan to jokingly kiss her, too, just as she'd predicted—and with a perfectly-timed flick of the wrist, she opened her fan in front of her face. Bach Duong leaned forwards, eyes closed, and Xuan Thu watched as he gave the paper a tender kiss. His eyes flew open in confusion, and he stepped back with an embarrassed cough. The Luu family's middle daughter was no joke.

But while Bach Duong was arrogant and had a habit of imposing himself upon others, he was not one of the Monstrous Eighteen.

To know who Bach Duong was, one only needed to listen to the story that he told next, with all the glitz that came with it. Bach Duong lived to impress, to be flashy, to be the best. Even the simplest question would turn into some thrilling and complicated monologue on his part, and he would never pass up the chance to tell his dramatic life history.

Bach Duong, he began to explain, was the son of General Bach, the great military leader.

Bach Duong's story had begun twenty years before, when General Bach had been fighting on foreign land. Top-secret information had been leaked by some dishonest courtier and left the general's army besieged. His entire army was slaughtered—almost. Only one man stood by him, fighting his way through. Despite this man's small frame, he managed to save the general's life from their vicious enemies.

Appreciating his savior's abilities, and given his mortal debt, the two of them became sworn brothers. On the long journey home they went through thick and thin, just the two of them. Strong and resourceful, General Bach was left in indescribable awe of his new brother-in-arms, Dianthus.

Not long after they swore their pact of brotherhood, General Bach discovered Dianthus wasn't a man at all, but was in fact a woman disguised as a soldier.

It was a shocking revelation, but the general had developed feelings for Dianthus beyond those of their "brotherhood." Instead of condemning her for the crime, General Bach concealed it and promised that when they returned to the imperial city, he would make her his second wife. The two were pursued by enemies over the thousands of miles it took to journey home—and by the time they got close to the imperial city, Dianthus' due date was also closing in.

Once again, so close to home, they fell under the attack of the courtiers who had betrayed them. One night, the two stopped their horses at a small village. Dianthus noticed that the village seemed too quiet: it was nighttime, yet there was neither light nor smoke coming out from the houses. But the two were exhausted, and the child in Dianthus' womb had started kicking, so they decided to enter the village despite their misgivings.

As they walked into the square at the center of town, the sounds of rushing drums filled the air. Enemy soldiers appeared in droves and surrounded them from all sides. Swords and spears flew, and torches lit up the sky. The two once again fought courageously to open up an escape route.

General Bach took hit after hit, but, even wounded, they managed to escape—only to find themselves cornered at the bottom of a huge canyon.

With no other option, General Bach and Lady Dianthus left their horses behind them. Panting and stumbling, they clung to each other as they scrambled up into the mouth of a cave in the canyon wall. The stone was wet and mossy, and the entrance so narrow that Lady Dianthus almost couldn't pass through with her swollen belly.

Inside, it was a lovely pink color, and they found a tastefully decorated room.

In the middle of the room sat a woman idly playing a dan tranh, a plucked zither. She seemed middle-aged, but her clothes and fingernails were colored with a bright and youthful pink. The woman didn't stop playing even after seeing the injured couple creep in. Instead, she calmly continued performing the soothing piece to her new audience.

General Bach and Lady Dianthus knelt down before her. "We didn't mean to intrude. But we are lost, and outside, our enemies have caught up to us. Lady, please let us take refuge for a night."

"There is warm water inside; you should take a bath and rest," the lady said, without looking up. Her voice blended into the music like a song. She then changed her melody to one unlike any the couple had heard before, and the music opened a hidden door in the cave wall, revealing yet another secret room.

General Bach and Dianthus thanked her, happy to have finally found a stroke of luck, and helped each other inside. Just as they disappeared into the cave, their pursuers swarmed in. Soldiers ransacked the cave, overturning every piece of furniture with no care for the damage they were doing.

The lady in pink merely played her zither without saying a word: the soldiers couldn't discover the hidden door.

After the failed inspection they turned and prepared to retreat.

Suddenly the cry of an infant echoed throughout the cave: as soon as Dianthus had entered the secret chamber, she'd gone into a quick labor. The newborn baby cried impressively loudly, considering his small lungs. The soldiers tracked his cry, destroyed the wall, and aggressively tore the infant from Dianthus' hands, throwing him violently toward the ground.

It was only then that the pink lady stopped her performance.

Her whole body began to glow pink as a hot coal.

The aura formed a halo, catching the infant and keeping him floating in midair.

The lady's chi brightened into a bright, sparkling pink, and the stone cave suddenly burned hot as a furnace. The pink silk ribbons on the wall curled and blackened, the zither on the table was eaten up in flame, and the strings of the instrument snapped, one by one. The soldiers turned into living torches. Only General Bach, Dianthus, and the infant, wrapped in pink energy by the lady, were unharmed.

Her blistering power exploded from the cave and radiated for miles and miles, and the enemy soldiers stationed outside were incinerated instantly.

Both General Bach and Dianthus knew about the Whispered World, and after that display, they looked at each other in terror.

"Isn't this the legendary Solar Radiance...?"

The lady, who would later call herself Lady Pink, nodded and smiled.

"I am a hermit who just wants to practice martial arts, and yet you two led each other in. I have been practicing Solar Radiance, a martial art used for mass killing and nothing else, for a very long time. I had never used it. But today, the first time it was used, it saved an infant! What a miracle!"

"A fortunate child born in the cave of Lady Pink! This must be the will of the gods. You saved his life, Lady Pink. You should become his godmother!" Dianthus exclaimed.

General Bach invited the lady to the capital so that he could have the opportunity to show his gratitude, but Lady Pink just smiled and pulled a new zither from the wall to replace the one that had burned to charcoal in her hands.

"I don't like lavish places. You two should go. When this child turns ten years old, I will meet him and teach him the arts."

General Bach and Lady Dianthus were overjoyed. After saying goodbye, they promised to welcome her in ten years.

"And that child...was young master Bach?!" the whole dojo asked in unison: everyone was in awe of the child's dramatic past.

"Nope." Bach Duong shook his head. "Not me."

They all stared in exasperation.

"So what does that child have to do with you, that you forced everyone to listen to that story, young master Bach?"

Bach Duong sure knew the art of wasting other people's time.

"Be patient!" Bach Duong reassured them, and glanced around the room leisurely, with sparkling eyes, before continuing.

The infant was named Phong. From the moment he had been born, he'd absorbed the energy of the miraculous Solar Radiance. And, after ten years, Lady Pink had accepted him as her sworn son. His future had been as bright as the sun.

When General Bach returned to the capital, he learned that his first wife, Lien, had gotten pregnant before he had left for war, and had given birth to a son named Duong. Both were beautiful children, and General Bach had been indescribably happy.

Lien was an understanding, mild and meek person. She accepted Lady Dianthus and loved Bach Phong as her own child. Lien cared about Dianthus; she understood that since Dianthus was used to roaming the Whispered World, living in the palace and being subjected to its many rituals and prejudices would put her under a lot of pressure.

And indeed, whatever she tried, Lady Dianthus still became more and more bored with the restrictive royal life. And, because she had to share her loved one with Lien, gradually her love for General Bach faded. Although the relationship between Lien and Dianthus was companionable, the relationship between Dianthus and General Bach no longer felt as passionate as it had been out in the world.

Eventually, Lady Dianthus locked herself in her room all day, looking at the sky through the window like a bird in a cage. So it was that before he was even able to speak, Bach Phong already had a huge responsibility on his shoulders. He had tied his freedom-loving mother down; he had caged that beautiful bird.

As Lady Dianthus faded from their lives, Lien took over raising both children alone. During the yearly mid-autumn festival, when Phong was five, she took the two children to the garden to play with the paper lanterns. That night the full moon shone particularly brightly. The children ate cake, drank tea, and happily chased each other around the garden, gripping the paper lanterns in their grubby hands.

"Brother, there is a strange sound in the lotus pond," Phong said, and, despite the other boy's protests, curiously dragged Bach Duong to the pond. The night was quiet; there was only the sound of the fish lightly breaking the surface of the water, which reflected the bright, yellow moon like a mirror. Afraid that the children would fall in as they looked at the water, Lien stepped a little closer.

Suddenly a black figure emerged from the pond. It grabbed Bach Phong and dragged him into the water, and Lien, driven by instinct, quickly caught hold of his leg—but she was a delicate woman, and the two were pulled downwards together. They fell into the water, but curiously, the lotus pond remained as calm as a mirror, silently reflecting the moon without a ripple.

Bach Duong screamed. The servants ran for help, and soldiers in the palace rushed over. People jumped into the pond, searching for the missing, and this time, the surface broke. In the morning, only Lien's body was found, floating facedown among the white lotus flowers. Bach Phong was nowhere to be found.

Hearing the news that her son Bach Phong was dead without a trace, and that her friend Lien had lost her life trying to save him, Lady Dianthus abandoned the General's household.

Lien died, Phong disappeared, and Dianthus left with no goodbyes. In just one night, General Bach's family fell to pieces. And Bach Duong witnessed the whole thing from start to finish, standing right next to Bach Phong when his younger brother was dragged into the water.

The image of Bach Phong and his mother falling into the pond never faded from his mind. It was burned onto the back of his eyelids. The arm that had pulled Bach Phong down into the dark water was marked by three black streaks, intertwined like a rope.

Five years later, Lady Pink came to find Bach Phong, but he was no longer at the palace. Sympathizing with the pain of General Bach, she accepted Bach Duong as her disciple instead. Years passed. Bach Duong grew up; he inherited the extraordinary strength of his father and the attractiveness of his mother, and he learned martial arts from Lady Pink— now Grandma Pink—of the Monstrous Eighteen.

"Because of that, I'm completely fluent in both martial arts and literature, and I'm also of a noble bloodline that is admired by many people. I learned martial arts from Grandma Pink, but I am a person full of personality and glamour, still retaining my own style, never once wearing pink clothes like she requested!" Bach Duong revealed dramatically. Upon hearing that, the school's members glanced at each other, eyebrows raised. Bach Duong's lack of self-awareness really was extraordinary.

Even so, under that perfect outward appearance, Bach Duong was still haunted by the traumatic events that had happened that day. Since childhood he had always wanted to investigate the monster in the lotus pond that had brought his mother and brother to their watery graves; but it had always been forbidden by Grandma Pink.

That had remained true until the day Grandma Pink called Bach Duong in for an audience. Her room was decorated with the usual pink, but this time there were seven beautiful women in white waiting.

"Bring back my Storm Pearl," she said without preamble, her voice deep and resonant. "The Storm Pearl was found by me and one other person…"

This person, Samsara of the Poison Legion, was a dishonest, devilish woman. Grandma Pink inherently possessed profound inner powers, and Samsara of the Poison Legion was also transcendent and skilled at many evil arts. The two women had not merely been sworn sisters; they had been lovers, and they'd combined their powers to search the Whispered World for the Storm Pearl.

"I just wanted to learn martial arts. Finding the Pearl would help me hone my inner power," Grandma Pink explained. "Samsara had…other intentions. When she found the Storm Pearl, not only did she take it away, but she struck me in the back. I was engulfed in demonic flame. The blow left me unable to walk, but the pain of my partner's betrayal was worse. Samsara left me for another woman, and then she founded the Poison Legion, of which she claims to be the matriarch," the woman went on. "She has hundreds of disciples underneath her who only do evil deeds. One of the most powerful leaders of the Poison Legion is called Obsidian. There is black snow in every step he takes."

"Black snow in every step? Beautiful, isn't it?" Bach Duong had commented admiringly. "But can it be possible? How can a normal person be constantly surrounded by snow?"

There hadn't been many people who had faced Obsidian and walked out alive, so the legend of the snow could have been a rumor of the Whispered World. Upon hearing the rumors, only Grandma Pink understood: the black snow and the cold energy were real. They existed only in those who had swallowed the Pearl and successfully cultivated the Storm Strike.

"Take these seven women with you. Kill Obsidian and bring me the Storm Pearl!" Grandma Pink had ordered.

That order also meant that Bach Duong, who had mastered his martial arts, could take his place and lead. First, he would bring the Storm Pearl to Grandma Pink; and then he would find out the identity of the person who'd murdered Phong and Lien. Upon hearing the order, Bach Duong had shouted with great joy.

Knowing Samsara of the Poison Legion inside and out, Grandma Pink passed down many methods to neutralize disciples of the Poison Legion. Bach Duong had the antidote for the toxins on Obsidian's skin. If he drank it, even if he were poisoned, he could still keep his life—something that could be said by no other.

That was the antidote Bach Duong had given to Dong Tu that night.

"I want to find Obsidian," Dong Tu said, after listening closely to everything.

A small stab of disappointment struck Bach Duong. After telling such a tragic family story, Dong Tu still only cared about *him*.

"Obsidian was seriously injured because of me. In this world, no one else can touch or heal him! I must look for him!" Dong Tu worried.

"Especially when he kissed you so passionately!" Anole nodded.

"Kissed? When?" Dong Tu demanded, startled.

"While you were unconscious. Oh, what a magnificent sight! Lips on lips, eyes closed, enjoying the sweet taste of love!" Switch added.

Xuan Thu and Bao Thuong had to nod their heads, even if they didn't want to. It was true. The incident was being portrayed by the Monstrous Three in an overly dramatic way, but Obsidian had indeed kissed Dong Tu.

"Come to think of it, it was very romantic. It looked like you were kissing him back, too! But you don't remember anything! What a pity!" Xuan Thu shook her head sympathetically.

Bao Thuong glowered. He'd been beside Dong Tu for many years. He'd wanted to kiss her every moment he was around her, but hadn't dared to. Meanwhile, this *Obsidian* guy had blatantly kissed her in front of everyone while she was *dead!*

"Besides, Dong Tu, you're considered dead. It's not possible for you to stay at the dojo," Xuan Thu pointed out. "I'll go too!"

"No, Miss Xuan Thu!" Bao Thuong interjected. "Without being trained, you can't run around the Whispered World! Let me go with them!" Obviously, going with Dong Tu would give him the chance to get closer to her, to...well, to...protect her from the guy who had suddenly held her so passionately! Yes. That was the one.

"Dong Tu and Bao Thuong, you two are both proficient in martial arts, but you are naive and foolish," Xuan Thu insisted. "If I don't go with you, you could meet...criminals! Who will scam you out of all of your money!"

Bach Duong agreed to let Xuan Thu accompany them, still bitter. He had never been denied a kiss before meeting her!

"But we don't know where to start," Dong Tu sighed.

"That Obsidian guy was seriously injured, so he will probably crawl back to that sassy girl," Anole guessed. As soon as he finished that sentence, he caught a sharp look from Switch.

"Which sassy girl?" Dong Tu asked nervously.

"Your *rival*," Switch smirked. "The evil woman that Obsidian always runs back to: Ivy of Hoa Hon Palace, a spoiled little minx!"

Upon hearing that, Dong Tu suddenly recalled the fingernail marks on Obsidian's arms and shoulders. Her body became as hot as fire, and blood rushed to her face.

The Emperor's Order

"Why waste your precious time looking for Ivy? You should follow me to learn martial arts." Startling everyone, the Stargazer seemed to appear out of nowhere.

"This is not your business, old lady." The other eccentric masters hadn't expected her to be interested in this sort of drama.

"You're too late. You missed all the excitement!" Switch pouted.

"An old woman like me doesn't want to intrude in places where there's fighting," the Stargazer countered. "Besides, on my way here, while I was eating some spring rolls, I foresaw what would happen. So I had no need to rush." She had tracked the stars to monitor the incident; she was the Stargazer, after all.

"Obsidian is so stubborn," she continued. "I told him to watch out for the arrow, but he never listens."

"Stargazer, could you please tell me where to find Obsidian?" Dong Tu asked hesitantly. She admired the old woman's abilities, even if the others seemed to scoff at her.

"You and that man are destined to meet each other again, don't worry. But you two are not meant to be together. Even reuniting will bring you injury and separation. If you find and bring me a fragment of the Sunlight Pearl, I will take you as my student and train you, so that you might reforge your destiny. Otherwise, you two will lead treacherous lives."

"How can you teach martial arts when you haven't been trained?" Switch muttered. "You're only good at a few wild guesses."

"While I don't have the same skills, I do know what kind Dong Tu needs to learn!" The old Stargazer seemed certain beyond all doubt. Looking down her nose at Bach Duong, she contemptuously said, "And you, if you want to settle your family's feud, forget about the Storm Pearl. Instead, go get the fragments of the Sunlight Pearl for me."

She seemed to hate Bach Duong. Dong Tu wondered if it was because he had kissed her in the past.

"Not a chance!" Bach Duong shouted. "What is this Sunlight Pearl everyone's looking for anyway?"

"The Sunlight Pearl is a beautiful pearl that matches the color of my skin." The old woman smiled mischievously. "Compared to it, the Storm Pearl you people are scrambling to acquire will be nothing but a worthless piece of rock."

"An old woman with no martial arts training has no need for the Storm Pearl. Your desire for that Sunlight Pearl fragment doesn't mean we have to find it!" Anole told her. Stargazer or not, he was convinced the old woman was senile.

"Thank you for such wise words," Dong Tu said gently. "I just want to find Obsidian to see how his injuries are and express my gratitude to him. My intentions have nothing to do with romance or with finding this Sunlight Pearl."

"Well then, it's up to you. But don't you blame me for this," the old woman snapped, feigning annoyance. She couldn't say she hadn't seen it coming. "You can mess around and learn what you want. Just don't forget the Sunlight Strike Technique! Your fate with Obsidian depends on it." She composed herself and gave them all a regal glare. "Now I need to get some sleep."

The gathered group watched as she scuttled out.

The old Stargazer had appeared and spoken of some obscure prophecies, but only one was worthwhile to most of the group—her last line about going to bed. By then everyone had noticed that it was almost morning. They were all tired, and it showed on their lined faces. One by one they left for their rooms to rest.

The Monstrous Three—Leatherback, Anole, and Switch—gathered into a room.

Leatherback, normally able to fall asleep easily and be snoring as soon as he lay down, was restless despite his exhaustion.

"Anole, Switch, are you guys really going to escort Dong Tu to Hoa Hon Palace and find Ivy?" he asked, finally giving in and breaking the silence.

"Of course. It's been a while. I wonder if Lady Ivy will be any prettier!" Anole replied enthusiastically.

Switch pouted at Anole's excitement about the idea. She scratched at the ugly, cracked skin on her cheek.

"Dong Tu really likes Obsidian," she said. "And—he kissed her. So Dong Tu and Ivy meeting ought to be fun!"

"I will not allow it," Leatherback said. "You two are great at fighting, and messing with the people of Hoa Hon Palace is your own choice. But Dong Tu is still just an ordinary girl. Don't foolishly toy with her to just waste a human life! Besides, Obsidian is powerful, and a member of the Poison Legion. You should know their rules well enough. A relationship between Obsidian and Dong Tu will bring no good."

"You think it's better not to pair Obsidian with Dong Tu, huh?" Anole mused. "That might be true. There's only a little infatuation between them. It should be over soon. Letting the string tighten between them will only hurt them even more."

"Since when did you become such a softie? We three have always gotten ourselves into other people's drama just for the fun of it. Why are you suddenly being so nice?" Switch snapped, then softened her voice into a sweet whisper. "We're just offering to help get those two lovebirds together. Build a bridge, erase the line, stoke a little fire...what's wrong with that? If they love each other and the situation separates them, that's their business!"

Switch had sworn not to believe in love, but her mind still clung to the idea. She still hoped something would come along to prove her wrong. The more she understood that Obsidian and Dong Tu would have many obstacles, the more she wanted to bring the two of them together, if only to test the power of love. If the two fought to be together and failed, she would laugh because she had already won—love wasn't everything.

On the other hand, if the two of them overcame all their obstacles, she wouldn't feel so stupid for hoping that, one day, she would eventually find the love of her life. No matter what happened, Switch would be satisfied.

It didn't take long for Leatherback to figure out that Switch was going to try and deliberately create a tragedy to test their hearts. He was also sure that Obsidian and Dong Tu's relationship would go nowhere, and it concerned him. In his rare moment of goodness, he wanted to stop Switch's cruel joke immediately—no matter how funny it might turn out to be. Stopping her was his first priority.

Anole didn't take the warnings as seriously as Switch or Leatherback. He just cared about taking Dong Tu to Hoa Hon Palace to meet Ivy and getting the chance to admire Ivy's beauty.

The three wanderers whispered, and the whispers turned to regular gossip, and then they began to quarrel loudly, and eventually they began to fight. The old hunchback pulled out his bronze bell and beat Switch with it; Switch used her chi to make her hands hot and fuming. Anole stood in the middle to defend for one person even as he helped the other, which just made the other two eccentric masters fight harder. The fight only stopped when Leatherback tore off Switch's face and threw it at Anole. The two squealed in frustration, Switch demanding her face back.

That seemed to be the end of it; except, when the sun marked well past noon, Leatherback realized that Switch and Anole had secretly fled with Dong Tu. Anole and Switch had known that the old hunchback would continue to badger them, so they had snuck out early.

As for Dong Tu, she hadn't wanted to drag Xuan Thu and Bao Thuong into her business, and she couldn't stand the idea of having Bach Duong along, so she left quietly, leaving only a farewell letter.

Xuan Thu read the letter to everyone at the dojo, anxiety twisting in her belly. She was especially upset when she saw that this Leatherback character was so angry that he left without saying a word.

Meanwhile, the sounds of many marching feet began to filter in from outside; Vinh Phuc's men were encircling the dojo, surrounding the school. Two rows of soldiers marched their way into the hall, paving the way for eight people hauling a heavy wooden palanquin.

The Luu family was frightened. Could the magistrate have discovered that Dong Tu's death had been faked? The girl was gone and the coffin was empty. What if he wanted to examine the body? How would they deal with him? Even a smart person like Xuan Thu didn't know what to do next. She wondered if Bach Duong, as the son of a great general from the court, could manage to help them.

"I can't." Bach Duong shrugged. "I went out to mingle with the common folk. Unnecessarily taking advantage of my authority will create a bad reputation for my family. Let's see what they want first."

Everything seemed about to get worse. The magistrate came to the dojo. He wasn't even the one sitting on that palanquin; he was on foot all the way, and once he was inside, they were greeted by his stern face.

"All kneel!" the magistrate shouted.

89

The soldiers pounded their spears on the ground in unison with a loud bang. The entire Luu family, including Xuan Thu, kneeled down right away, but Bach Duong and the seven women blatantly stayed on their feet.

A person in front of the palanquin saw this and marched over to him.

"Sir Bach Duong, you have a decree from the emperor. Will you kneel and receive the emperor's message?"

Bach Duong was shocked when the man before him dropped the fan he'd been holding in front of his face. The man was in his forties, short, and wore a touch of blush on his pale cheeks. He wore a colorfully embroidered silk dress, and he looked nothing short of majestic. As he folded the fan, Bach Duong immediately recognized who he was, and he signaled the seven women to kneel down.

"Eunuch Trinh!" Bach Duong bowed his head.

Trinh raised his hand, and the entire army of the Vinh Phuc district retreated outside. One by one, they left the hall, with only a small group to accompany the palanquin. Trinh waved his fan, and someone from behind him stepped forward to present a shiny golden scroll. In a solemn and powerful voice, he read aloud the contents of the scroll.

The emperor wanted Bach Duong, Son of General Bach, to allow a young eunuch called Thien Thien, who was close to Princess Thien Binh, to travel with them—and for Bach Duong try his best to protect Thien Thien.

Bach Duong grew more annoyed the more he heard. One of the seven women, Friday, nudged his hip.

"Sir Bach Duong, keep smiling!" Friday reminded Bach Duong, quietly pointing out his displeased expression.

Xuan Thu sighed with relief. Vinh Phuc's ferocious troops had come to the dojo, not because of Dong Tu, but because of Bach Duong.

By the time Trinh had finished reading the emperor's edict, he gestured for the men to lift up the palanquin curtain for Thien Thien to step out.

Xuan Thu found it strange that a powerful old eunuch like Trinh had to show such respect to a young eunuch like Thien Thien. That little eunuch held such importance that the emperor had sent out an army to seek out Bach Duong. It wasn't clear how Thien Thien, Princess Thien Binh, and Bach Duong were related, but nevertheless, Bach Duong was to protect and escort Thien Thien throughout their journey.

Xuan Thu was not a noble. She wasn't very familiar with eunuchs. But when Thien Thien stepped out of the palanquin, Xuan Thu knew there was something off. The eunuch had his servant pull up the curtain of the palanquin, and then turned his backside to bend out and stepped on the cloth dangling from the palanquin, nearly letting his hat fall off. He quickly grabbed the hat, set it properly on his head, and adjusted his shirt as he stood straight.

Little eunuch Thien Thien was the same height as Dong Tu and Xuan Thu. He was delicate and slender, with a feminine air. His blasé attitude made him look haughty. He had a round face, narrow eyes, and small, petal-blossom lips adorned with a thin layer of light pink lipstick. His long nails were painted a light pink color.

Xuan Thu eyed him skeptically. He was a man, but his body was as slender as a girl's, with a long, soft neck. A unique scent surrounded him: even the elegant and fancy Bach Duong didn't smell so good.

Thien Thien cleared his throat, imitating the gesture of a true eunuch, and said, "Sir Bach Duong! My name is Thien Thien, Princess Thien Binh's servant. Thank you for letting me accompany you. I am under your protection now."

Thien Thien bowed his head, but glanced mischievously at Bach Duong. Unlike Xuan Thu, Bach Duong wasn't observant; he hadn't noticed any of the oddities in the eunuch's appearance or bearing. He reluctantly accepted his mission.

Thien Thien had a flashy gait, theatrical and willowy. It was like an invisible aura exuded from him and overshadowed Bach Duong. Until then, Bach Duong had only been surrounded by women; now he'd have this eunuch accompanying him. Just looking at Thien Thien frustrated the larger man.

THE GIRL WHO KEPT WINTER

The whole group set out to search for Obsidian. Xuan Thu begged to go along to find Dong Tu. It would have been a good opportunity for Bach Duong to kiss Xuan Thu, but the presence of Thien Thien killed any desire he had. Bao Thuong also insisted on following them, but was bluntly refused by Bach Duong.

So the party, consisting of Bach Duong, his seven women in their shining white clothes, the mysterious eunuch Thien Thien, and Xuan Thu, hurriedly took their leave of the Luu family to begin their journey. None of them knew where Hoa Hon Palace was located, and the old Stargazer had at first been reluctant to give them directions, but eventually she had told them vaguely to head west, so that was what they did.

The group enjoyed the scenery as they walked. Thien Thien and Xuan Thu were not used to going on long trips, so they had to stop to eat and rest more often. Thien Thien seemed like a child who was going out for the first time: whenever he saw anything unfamiliar, his curiosity got the best of him, which meant their journey progressed painfully slowly. Bach Duong kept cursing the little eunuch under his breath.

The group stopped at a tea house for the rest of the afternoon.

The ten-person group took up almost the entire space, and Bach Duong ordered every dish the tea house offered for his ladies to enjoy. The owner swirled in and out. Within a minute, the table was filled with numerous hearty dishes. The girls happily stirred the rice, serving Bach Duong and each other. Thien Thien put his chopsticks together and waited to see who would serve him his food, but nobody paid him any attention. Watching Bach Duong give some food to Xuan Thu frustrated him, and he used his chopsticks to fight for his share.

While Bach Duong's table was bustling, in the corner there was a calmer one. Sitting there alone was a young wandering swordsman, wearing ragged clothes and without any belongings. On his table lay an ordinary-looking sword. The swordsman was young and strong, but it was clear by his lankiness that he had yet to finish growing into his broad shoulders. Fresh-faced and bright-eyed, with a square chin, wide forehead, and thick brows, he was at the age when he should have been eating constantly to catch up to his bones—and yet he'd only ordered a small steamed bun and a cup of tea, and he ate his meal slowly.

The swordsman chipped away at the single steamed bun for a long time, quietly and meditatively. For anyone studying martial arts, the most important thing was meditation. Yet Bach Duong had come in and unintentionally caused a stir: it didn't take long for the pleasant smell of food to find its way to the young swordsman's nose. He frowned, wiped his nose, and turned his back so that the seductive smell of the chicken and stir-fried vegetables with garlic wouldn't linger. But he couldn't escape the delicious aroma of those dishes, waking up a stomach that had been rumbling for many days: the poor swordsman couldn't afford to order more food.

From a distance of two steps away, Bach Duong also heard the groan of the swordsman's stomach. The girls giggled and laughed together. Thien Thien blankly looked around without any clue as to what the rumbling sound was; perhaps no one in the emperor's court had ever heard or made such a growling sound.

Xuan Thu sympathized with the swordsman, who was blushing, holding a hand over his stomach to keep it from growling. Bach Duong whispered in the owner's ear and ordered some food for the swordsman.

As soon as the food arrived at his table, the swordsman devoured all of it eagerly; then he went to Bach Duong's table to greet him.

"Thank you, my lords and ladies! Please allow me to know your names. Thank you for offering me food, and for the great kindness you show to such a commoner like me."

Bach Duong and his people each introduced themselves. The swordsman repeated each name and remembered it clearly in his heart. After that, he also introduced himself.

"I lost my parents when I was very young, so I really don't know my family name. Please just call me Phong," he requested. "I have been traveling to the Collector's Hall to see the man who possesses the Storm Pearl. Where are you all heading?"

Needless to say, Bach Duong was tremendously interested in this newcomer.

CHAPTER 7

Phong

The members of Bach Duong's famously chivalrous group immediately took a liking to the poor swordsman. Grateful for Bach Duong's generous gesture, he talked with the group while he wolfed down dessert.

As time went on, Bach Duong discovered not just that Phong was an orphan, and had lost his parents during his childhood, but that his memories of the past were fuzzy. His earliest memory, Phong explained, was being rescued by a martial arts master, Luc Can Huy—who went by the title Myo Pic.

Bach Duong tipped his head in interest.

"Is there a black scar braided like a rope on your master's wrist?" he questioned.

"If there was, I didn't notice any black mark...but it is true that my master's weapon is a rope," Phong replied, scratching his ear absentmindedly.

"I would like to meet your master," Bach Duong told him, torn between hope and skepticism. Phong would be about the same age as Bach Phong, his younger brother, if his brother were still alive; and if his master used a rope as his weapon of choice, he would likely have scarred himself from its use over the years.

"Master is also on his way to the Collector's Hall," Phong said in response. "Just come along and you'll meet him! We got word that the Collector has captured the deviant who possesses the Storm Pearl. In a few days there will be a banquet to show them off; he plans to make the man perform the Storm Strike for everyone to watch. It's never been seen before!" Phong grinned at Bach Duong's group, excited at the prospect of such a show.

Thien Thien clapped his hands excitedly. "Let's go! This is the chance of a lifetime—we can't pass it up."

The other members agreed wholeheartedly: the Storm Strike was not to be missed.

Xuan Thu had been quiet up to that point. She thought to herself, *if this stranger at the Hall is Obsidian, I wonder if Dong Tu knows it and found her way there. But she would be surrounded by hordes of people—how could she rescue Obsidian?*

Xuan Thu worried about her sister relentlessly, making Dong Tu—miles away—sneeze again and again.

As it turned out, Dong Tu was a few days' walk in the opposite direction from Bach Duong's group and the poor swordsman Phong. Anole and Switch were leading her to the gate of Hoa Hon Palace.

In fact, Hoa Hon Palace was quite close to the east of the Luu family's dojo. It was ruled by Lady Ivy, who, according to Anole and Switch, had a "very intimate relationship" with Obsidian. On the outside, they were similar: Lady Ivy's body was pure poison and deadly to the touch, just like Obsidian's. Inwardly, however, her heart was a thousand times more cruel. Lady Ivy, alone in her realm, had built up Hoa Hon Palace not only to craft her poison, but also to relax with Obsidian in her leisure time.

The more Dong Tu heard about their story, the more she thought of those peculiar scratches on Obsidian's shoulders, and it made her heart race.

The path to Hoa Hon Palace ran through the countryside, remote and difficult to travel. The trio followed the path into a dense forest. The canopy overhead was thick and overgrown, with only a few shafts of sunlight piercing the leaves to streak in ethereal columns of light to the ground below. As they moved deeper in, however, the lush green vegetation began to die away; instead, sickly skeletons of trees and bushes dotted the landscape, the brittle branches bare and stark. By the time there was no living vegetation left, they had reached the center of the forest and come to a large, steel-colored lake. An island sat in the center, swathed in mist, and from a distance it looked as if it were floating on a cloud.

The trio looked at each other.

"Hoa Hon Palace is on that island, isn't it?" Dong Tu asked. Anole and Switch nodded grimly. They found a boat tied at the shoreline and rowed through the thickening mist to the island. Once they reached it, they had to climb up hundreds of stone steps in that unnatural fog. The island was hazy and seemingly devoid of human life: only scorpions and centipedes crawled all over the ground––not to mention the silhouettes of venomous snakes curled up in the mist as if waiting for something on the steps.

By the time Switch, Anole, and Dong Tu arrived in front of Hoa Hon Palace's old, rusted metal gate, the sunset had dappled their shadows with a deep purple hue.

The island was fearfully silent as Anole approached the gate to pound on it. The heavy metal gate creaked open, and a servant dressed entirely in black, only his eyes exposed, peeked out. He looked as though he had blended himself into the twilit shadows.

"My name is Luu Dong Tu," Dong Tu introduced herself. "I'm from the Luu School of Martial Arts. I would like to meet Lady Ivy. I—"

The servant began to close the door, disregarding the strange guests.

"Tell that little brat that this lady here is Obsidian's wife. She comes to look for her husband!" Switch interrupted, folding her arms. The servant's starkly visible eyes widened in fright. He turned and rushed inside. Meanwhile, Dong Tu blushed furiously; before she could have a chance to correct Switch's bold statement, the gate was thrown open wide for them to enter. Inside were many servants, every one covered from head to toe in black.

Their clothes...this must be the right place, Dong Tu thought to herself. *The hostess of the palace is full of poison, so wearing clothes like that might help protect them.*

Protected from poison or not, the servants were to be pitied, because the palace was as hot as a furnace. The air smelled strongly of herbs, thick with the smoke of incense. The servants pointed at Dong Tu, whispering to each other with downcast eyes. Anole and Switch quickly put on their gloves and masks. Switch whispered to Dong Tu in explanation.

"Ivy is very wicked. She can poison others by touching them. You may be able to survive her touch, but beware, do not take anything she offers!"

Dong Tu nodded her agreement.

They were taken to the main hall on a zigzagging path, from an herb garden to a study and then back to the yard. Every room was empty, hot, and smoky. Dong Tu wondered if there would be any end to their wanderings. Finally, another servant caught up with them and whispered to their guide.

"The mistress has entered—" he lowered his voice and winked–– "her lounge room to rest!"

Although they had been invited inside, Ivy was apparently ignoring her guests––hence the tour of the palace, in order to kill time. Dong Tu found her actions odd. Was it Ivy's intention to show off her palace, or was this just an unpleasant show of her personality?

Dong Tu, Anole, and Switch were led to a lounge room by the servant. The room was filled with dried flowers and herbs, and a curtained bed rested in its center. There was one particular scent wafting in the air with which Dong Tu was familiar: it reminded her of the curious scent that had surrounded Obsidian the night Dong Tu had cared for his wound.

Behind the chiffon curtains of the bed, Lady Ivy reclined and listened to the trio talk amongst themselves. Hearing words from the housekeeper, she moved the curtains and stepped out. Dong Tu was the first to notice her; although, just before the curtain dropped back to cover the bed, she saw another figure lying there.

Much to Dong Tu's surprise, Lady Ivy was mesmerizingly beautiful. She looked to be the same age as Dong Tu, or perhaps a few years older. Dong Tu took in her snow-white skin, long silken hair, glittering black eyes, and long, thick lashes. Her nose was small and perfect, her crimson lips heart-shaped. But it was not her beauty that startled Dong Tu the most.

In a shocking contrast to her servants, Ivy was almost completely naked.

Instead of clothing, she wore a large necklace made of many strands of sparkling stones. The chains and stones linked together, dangling down her body just barely to a length to cover her nipples. Around her waist she wore a string of pearls with many purple silk ribbons hanging from it; they flowed elegantly whenever Ivy moved. It not only highlighted the curves of her hips, but also revealed her inviting white thighs. Lady Ivy looked exactly like a jade statue abstaining clothing.

Dong Tu gulped. *She might look beautiful while motionless,* she thought, *but if she walked around the outside world in those so-called "clothes" it would shock everyone for miles.*

Lady Ivy stood up silently, circling the trio as if observing a strange creature. As she passed, Dong Tu noticed she had the same large black spider tattooed on her back as Obsidian.

Lady Ivy fixed her eyes on Dong Tu without blinking, her gaze incredibly spiteful. Dong Tu was still speechless. She looked at her companions for help; Anole was hungrily staring at the seductive Ivy, a drop of drool hovering on the edge of his mouth. Switch looked away with contempt.

"Have you come all the way here to find *my* Obsidian?" Ivy finally spat, emphasizing the word *my*. "He's way out of your league. No matter what happens, my Obsidian will never love *you!*"

"My lady, it never crossed my mind," Dong Tu said politely. She didn't want Ivy to misunderstand. "I owed Obsidian a favor, so I came here to express my gratitude, and I just wanted to know—"

"If he kissed Dong Tu passionately that day!" Switch cut in.

"Not that!" Dong Tu interjected quickly. "I just want to know how his injury is!" She tried to step on Switch's foot to warn her against speaking so boldly, but Switch easily dodged the warning stomp. She even lifted up her mask and stuck out her tongue at Dong Tu.

"Hmm..." Ivy gritted her teeth. "Do you really want to know how my dear Phong is, after what you did to him?" It was clear from her tone whom she referred to––Obsidian. Dong Tu felt a sudden sadness when Ivy affectionately used what must be his other name.

"That night, my Phong came back," Ivy said, delighting in Dong Tu's disappointment. "He was badly wounded and exhausted. He could not breathe, despite manipulating his own energy to heal his body. When I met him at the gate, he was unconscious. It was a miracle he managed to reach Hoa Hon Palace."

Ivy began to recount that terrible night. All the servants had frantically run to her in her lounge room, yelling out, "My lady, Obsidian is seriously injured! Come quickly!"

She'd followed them to the hall and saw the servants carrying Obsidian, whose body was covered in blood. Ivy had trailed behind the servants, calling out "Phong, my dear!" several times––but Obsidian had remained silent. His body was cold. Ivy had clasped his hand tightly, taking his pulse. It was barely present. It had terrified her.

"Call Samsara now! Sweet Phong, just stay strong!"

The palace fell into chaos that night, every servant running back and forth to fetch various items at Lady Ivy's request. She'd used her energy to take care of the wound on Obsidian's neck, but he had not stopped bleeding. The Sect Leader, Samsara herself, had rushed to the scene. They'd both continued to manipulate their power to heal Obsidian, using medicine and acupuncture on his body, along with every other technique they could think of. Even so, Obsidian had remained unconscious until the next morning.

Ivy had sat back on her heels, wiping sweat off her forehead.

"We can't do this, we can't heal him," she panted, terrified for her dear Phong's life. "We have to go beg for Thanh Nhan's help."

Samsara gritted her teeth, shouting back, "Why did you let this happen to him! Thanh Nhan is crafting her potions. If she knows about this, she will punish all of us!"

Thanh Nhan, of course, was the infamous Immortal Apothecarist of the Valley of Life and Death, the oldest woman among the Whispered World. Thanh Nhan the Immortal carried the power of resurrection, and was skilled in all kinds of poisons, injuries, and maladies. Asking her to save a life, however, came with a price: one had to try all seven of the most powerful poisons she could make. It would be no different than simply giving Thanh Nhan one's own life.

But Ivy had been desperate. She volunteered to take the punishment, begging Thanh Nhan to save Obsidian's life.

"The seven most lethal poisons," Ivy explained to the trio in the palace. "No one has ever survived after trying them. Even for the people of the Poison Legion, the seven poisons are a severe trial! No matter how familiar I am with all poisons, the seven were excruciatingly painful. But I had to save my wonderful Phong. I did not die. I'm too powerful to die."

Ivy paused in her story, showing her arm to Dong Tu. Her bare, snow-white arm was marred by many wounds, stings, bites, and bruises.

"And it was all because of you—you, who made me suffer this pain, trading my life to Thanh Nhan in exchange for Phong's life!" Ivy spat at Dong Tu. Her eyes showed the torment she had gone through as she continued to relate her story.

At last, Thanh Nhan had sent her apprentice to bring medicine for Obsidian. After three days, he regained consciousness. When he woke up, he could see what kinds of sacrifices Lady Ivy had made because of him.

Seeing her scars and her pain, he took her hand and said, "My Ivy–my dear! I will love you forever!"

Ivy narrated dramatically to her heart's content. The story nauseated Dong Tu, and tears brimmed at the edges of her lashes. She was so anxious about Obsidian's health. *I just want him to be safe,* she thought. At Ivy's last words, quoting Obsidian, she could not stop the tears from streaming down her cheeks.

In an odd gesture, Ivy walked over and gave Dong Tu a handkerchief to wipe her tears.

"You should go home now. Phong knows you're here, but he doesn't want to see you."

Dong Tu took the handkerchief gratefully. But as soon as she wiped her cheeks with it, her face began to tingle and turn red in splotches. Dong Tu remembered Switch's advice too late––never to touch anything Ivy offered. Their hostess chuckled quietly to herself.

"I am satisfied to know that Obsidian was healed after all of your dedicated care, Lady Ivy. I'll take my leave now." Dong Tu could barely contain the emotion in her words. She said her goodbyes to Ivy, then walked away, lost in thought. Anole and Switch ran after her.

They all left, Ivy watching gleefully from behind with a cunning smile.

"That was over the top." A hoarse voice spoke from the bed. Obsidian lifted the curtain to sit up. He was shirtless, his neck tightly bandaged. "I didn't say 'I love you forever'... and that bit about the seven poisons was a stretch. You can meet Thanh Nhan whenever you want. She immediately sent her apprentice to bring medicine here after she heard about my injury! And this arm..." Obsidian examined the wounds on Ivy's arm. "This was actually from fighting with—"

"Don't you really love me for the rest of your life?" Ivy retorted, pulling her hand back.

"Sure," Obsidian sighed, abandoning his questions. Ivy smiled widely, like a clever child.

"Plus, it was all because you wanted her to leave." She rushed to hug Obsidian, so tightly that he had to push her away because of his pain. She contented herself with embracing his arm, like a frog clasping onto a lotus branch. "You were absolutely right to want her to leave, though. We of the Poison Legion are not allowed to find love outside of the clan. My darling Phong is mine. Just mine!" Ivy bit her lip, remembering something from earlier. "Oh, wait a minute! Did you really kiss that girl?"

Obsidian pushed Ivy away.

"Stop it. Leave. I need to rest."

"You kissed a strange girl. I'm going to tell Samsara!"

Obsidian threw the blanket over his head in response.

"Phong," Ivy pestered, but Obsidian was determined to continue sleeping underneath his blanket. She reluctantly left him alone.

Outside, Dong Tu, who did not know Ivy had lied, found herself sobbing again.

"What's wrong?" Switch asked after they had caught up with her. Dong Tu had no answer. She felt the tears choke her throat.

Dong Tu was conflicted. Obsidian was a scoundrel. He had offered to help her escape from her wedding, and then suddenly kissed her without permission, and *then* he had been seriously injured, and now it turned out...he had an incredibly beautiful, seductive girlfriend. Dong Tu realized she had been stupid and foolish for the past few days, obsessively worrying over this man—who was also called Phong, apparently, which he hadn't even told her.

Since the day Obsidian had been injured, Dong Tu had felt like her soul was breaking into pieces every minute. She'd been fraught with anxiety the entire trip to Hoa Hon Palace. All that worrying just to find out that Obsidian had always been looked after by his beloved, self-sacrificing, beautiful Lady Ivy.

"Is that jealousy I'm sensing?" Switch asked.

"Not at all!" Dong Tu sniffled. After all, Obsidian had never said he liked Dong Tu.

"Then why are you crying?" Anole was unconvinced.

"Am I not allowed to cry?" Dong Tu asked. "It's smoky. My eyes hurt."

"Your heart's broken! Of course you can cry!" Switch exclaimed. "Traveling all the way to that forsaken place, just to look for the love of your life, and then finding out that he loves someone else! I would cry too."

Dong Tu ignored her.

"I was not looking for my lover in Hoa Hon Palace. I just wanted to say my thanks to Obsidian and ask how his injuries were. That's all! I'm not interested in him!"

"No?" Switch asked. "Then why haven't you done anything yet? You haven't met Obsidian to say thanks, and you haven't seen his condition either. All you did was listen to that wicked brat Ivy, and then you cried and ran away!"

Dong Tu bit her lip. Switch was right. *It* was *stupid of me to run away to cry just because of Lady Ivy's words*, she thought.

"We *have* come this far." Dong Tu stiffened her shoulders and wiped away her tears. "I can't just leave like this! I should know exactly what happened. I should hear it from Obsidian himself!"

Anole and Switch nudged each other, grinning mischievously. The Monstrous Pair cleared the way for Dong Tu to turn back, beating up any servants who tried to stop them, and they made the journey into Hoa Hon Palace once again.

CHAPTER 8

Obsidian

Hoa Hon Palace stood alone on the foggy island. The island itself was misty and fanciful, like a dream. Sunset merged with twilight as the purple sky mingled with the misty ground, turning the world into a surreal mirror of itself. The servants turned on the lights at the palace as night approached, and each light stood out in the fog as if it were a ghost. It was said that the word "Hoa" in the palace's name meant "painting." Indeed, it did look mysterious and beautiful, like a painting.

However, many people understood the word "Hoa" by a different meaning—"calamity." In that case, the fog was not beautiful; it was, in fact, made up of the souls of those who had died by Ivy's hand.

The palace was built in a circle, with four main corridors intersecting in a cross at the center. Underground and out of sight, the whole structure rested on a large and slowly rotating spindle. If one stood in place for a few hours, one could tell that the whole palace had rotated in a full circle.

The rooms and passages that swung around the center were designed to be confusing to outsiders: they were all nearly identical. Only residents of the island could find their way around.

Unfortunately, Dong Tu did not know the layout or design of the island. She simply turned around and walked back in the general direction of the palace. Anole and Switch, ahead of Dong Tu, were occupied with the struggling servants; as their backs were turned, Dong Tu disappeared into the mist, not knowing which block she turned down.

When the Monstrous Pair noticed that Dong Tu had disappeared, they met each other's eyes in panic. Ivy wasn't the only danger in Hoa Hon, and if Dong Tu did stumble back across Ivy, she no longer had their protection. It was only because of Anole and Switch that she had shown mercy and settled for giving Dong Tu the poisoned handkerchief.

More importantly, they had wanted to take Dong Tu back into the palace to watch the drama unfold––but now the main actor had wandered off! The two eccentric masters abandoned their pursuit of the servants and began to search for their companion.

Dong Tu retraced her steps, making her way back to Ivy's lounge room. Unbeknownst to her, however, the palace had twisted, and she was now in a completely different section. Arriving at a door, Dong Tu peeked inside what she thought was the lounge room.

Instead she found a room walled with bamboo clad in shining red copper, where many different types of weapons hung from the walls. From the ceiling draped large bamboo blinds on gold thread. The blinds formed winding paths within the room. Dong Tu coughed: this room was just as smoggy as the others. She realized she was not in Ivy's lounge and was about to turn around when she noticed a male figure standing in the middle of the room. Her curiosity got the better of her, and she took a step inside.

Through the bamboo curtain, Dong Tu saw that the young man was bare-chested and broad-shouldered. He wore a combination of pants and a skirt––tight leggings and two pieces of brocade to cover the front and back, with a large copper belt and a cuff on one arm. The man looked like a polished god from some mythical story, and he was muttering frustratedly to himself.

"These prostitutes...I touch them, and they all die! Now they're all dead, and none of them can do anything but just lie there!"

Dong Tu noticed the black spider tattoo on his shoulder blade with a start.

"Obsidian!" she called without thinking. Just as she recognized the tattoo, Dong Tu stumbled on something. She looked down.

It was a corpse.

The floor was littered with corpses. All of them were women, and they all appeared to have been poisoned just like she had. Dong Tu shrieked before she could stop herself.

The young man heard her cry and turned around. It was not Obsidian; his demeanor was equally cold, yet in a different way. He was a few years older than Dong Tu, and unlike Obsidian, whose cold was full of melancholy, this young man had a thick, fierce face. Down his whole left side ran black veins like a spiderweb, even webbing the skin from his forehead to the corner of his eye. It gave him an even harsher presence. Without the black veins, his face would have been quite beautiful, sharply angular and elegant. His eyes were lovely, hooded and shaped like willow leaves that curved gracefully upward, and his lips were straight and thin.

"Did you just call me Obsidian?" the man asked. "Because yes, I am he."

The imposter Obsidian's curious voice had the tone of a proud self-confession, as if the name Obsidian were some important title he longed for. He stalked the distance between himself and Dong Tu, grabbed her shirt, and jerked her in close. Dong Tu tried to fight her way out of his grip, but the man couldn't care less; all he noticed was that she was touching his body without being poisoned.

The implications of that thrilled him. For all his life, just like Obsidian, he had been unable to be touched without poisoning and killing those who even brushed against him.

The man threw Dong Tu over his shoulder and carried her through the blinds to a bed she hadn't been able to see before, dumping her unceremoniously on the mattress. Dong Tu scrambled across the bed to the corner.

"Stay away from me!" she warned. "If Obsidian knows you touched me like that, he'll—he'll—"

"What are you talking about? I am Obsidian, the King of Poison!" The stranger laughed, grabbing Dong Tu's shoulder to hold her still. He walked around to the side of the bed she'd crawled over to, bent, and rubbed his face against her cheek. "It feels so different to touch a living person!" Pouncing on the bed, the man dragged Dong Tu closer and ran his hands over every part of her he could reach, enthralled by the warmth of her body. Dong Tu struggled against his touch and managed to land a punch to his face. She fell off the bed, got her feet underneath her, and ran to the other side of the room, keeping her eyes on the man.

The imposter Obsidian scowled and wiped the blood from his nose. The scowl broke into a smirk and he snorted: the braver the girl, the more he liked the pursuit.

He reached for a vase of flowers on a table. Withdrawing a handful, he placed one stem sideways in his mouth. He plucked the petals from another flower, flicking them at

Dong Tu; the petals were thin, but the man threw them so forcefully that they were launched like darts. Dong Tu was able to dodge the first few petals, but after the fourth petal they began to pierce her shirt, pinning her to the wall and holding her fast.

"Help me! Anole! Switch!" Dong Tu shouted, but neither of her companions came. Instead, it was Lady Ivy who pushed open the door and entered the strange bamboo room.

"What's all this racket? My dear Phong is sleeping!" Ivy said. Seeing Dong Tu, she immediately became irritated. "This brat again! Why are you still here?"

"This is a friend of yours?" The man gestured toward Dong Tu.

Ivy shook her head.

"She's the one Phong likes! The wound on Phong's neck is because of *her*."

The man clapped his hands in amusement, crying out in a mocking voice:

"Is this really the girl Phong likes? Phong *likes* girls? I'm lucky tonight!"

"Please save me from him!" Dong Tu pleaded desperately.

But Lady Ivy turned to leave.

"Gia, remember to kill her afterwards. And don't let Phong know!"

"I know. He won't find out, believe me." The scarred man, apparently named Gia, nodded and smiled wickedly.

Ivy slammed the door shut behind her, paying Dong Tu no mind at all.

"Oh, and one more thing!" Ivy poked her head back in the room. "Don't let the brat scream. Phong is sleeping!" Again, the door slammed shut.

Gia approached Dong Tu, even more excited than before.

"Please don't kill me," she begged. "I just want to see Obsidian. Then I'll leave! I won't touch a thing!" Dong Tu was frantic. It was clear that even if she could have, Ivy would not have saved her.

"Kill you? Don't be worried about that! I won't kill you—yet," Gia reassured her. "As it turns out, Phong likes you, which is good!" A faraway look came into his eyes as he began to reminisce. "Ever since our childhood, Phong always fought and trained with me. We would hone our fighting skills, practicing every day to be the best. Ivy likes Phong more." Gia was bitter. "Our Leaders also valued Phong more. Phong is the only one, ever, to have mastered our sect's sacred teachings."

Gia remembered one such instance from long ago, and he began to recall the story to Dong Tu.

When he was young, the Poison Legion would abduct children, teaching them to be poison masters. Few children survived the ritual. Four of the most promising students of that year had been Phong, Gia, Ivy, and a young man named Truong. Gia and the other two had been born into the Poison Legion, while Phong had been brought in when he was nearly seven years old. Despite coming into the Legion later, Phong had learned and mastered the teachings much faster than Gia and Ivy.

Those four were the Poison Legion's top students. They had practiced fighting and using their chi and mastered the art of using poisons, both the poisons they created and the ones that laced their bodies. But Phong was the one who'd swallowed the Storm Pearl and successfully mastered the Storm Strike.

"Because he was the strongest?" Dong Tu blurted out.

"Wrong!" Gia said. "Truong was twenty-three years old, and Phong was only a teenager. Truong and I had both practiced with poisons for a long time, and our chi was far superior to Phong's! So much so, in fact, that..."

And Gia related that awful night when the four of them were taken to the main hall of the Poison Legion. Samsara and Thanh Nhan had ordered Thanh Nhan's personal assistant, Cassia, to fetch the Storm Pearl.

The Storm Pearl was the most legendary artifact in the world. Precious few had ever seen it. The tiny pearl contained immense powers, and it levitated on its own above the red velvet tray Cassia carried into the room. Whoever could absorb and wield the power of the Pearl would become unstoppable.

Truong and Gia could not contain their excitement at the sight of the treasure.

"You have completed your training," Thanh Nhan explained solemnly. "And now you must partake in the Trial of the Pearl. The Storm Pearl is our sect's most sacred relic; it will only bend to the one who is worthy of it."

Truong lifted his head in anticipation. Thanh Nhan continued.

"However, the Storm Pearl holds demonic energy. It is very selective of whom it trains with. In the past, those whom the Pearl deemed unfit have had their chi drained to nothing. Amongst the four of you, whoever can absorb the Pearl will become our clan's leader, the North King of Poison."

As the eldest and most powerful, Truong volunteered to test his worth first. He took a deep breath and focused, sinking into his chi and letting its warmth flow and fill him, a shield between him and the frozen power of the Pearl; only then did he set the Pearl on his tongue.

In an instant the Pearl thrummed, its icy power crackling against the warmth of his chi, Yin and Yang clashing in a vessel that was, as of yet, untested. He struggled to hold on, even as his breath curled and rushed from his lips in a snowy white cloud, and glittering frost blossomed across his skin in spiraling fractals.

Despite his struggling, Truong's skin darkened into a sickening, frozen, lifeless blue beneath the frost, and he felt his body begin to stiffen.

"Spit it out, brother!" Ivy screamed. Truong's eyes found hers as the Pearl's frost finally covered them—but it was too late.

By the time Ivy finished, Truong was nothing more than a frozen corpse.

Samsara leaned forward to touch him; Truong's snowy body crumbled into ice dust, and only the Storm Pearl remained, suspended in midair.

The three who remained were terrified.

Samsara turned to Thanh Nhan.

"Thanh Nhan, they are not ready yet. If they continue through the trial, they will die! We must wait a few years. Would that not be wiser?"

Thanh Nhan shook her head.

"We cannot wait another day. The destiny of the entire Poison Legion depends on this. If no one can foster the Storm Power, the Valley of Life and Death will..." Thanh Nhan stopped speaking, shaking her head as if to dispel the terrifying thought. She took a moment to compose herself. "The Storm Pearl is particular about the temperament of the person who contains its power. It doesn't depend on the person's skill with martial arts—only those who have the ability to absorb its negative energy will survive." Pointing at Phong, Thanh Nhan said, "Now it is your turn."

"Please, let me try!" Gia spoke up. Gia was a very confident and competitive person, and he'd held Truong in the utmost respect. If Truong could not become the king, then he had to try. He would not let Thanh Nhan make Phong the King of Poison.

Phong, on the other hand, did not like to compete. He stepped back, letting Gia take the Storm Pearl from their leader. Gia put the pearl in his mouth.

Back in the present, Gia blanched.

"The Storm Pearl is unnaturally cold," Gia said. "Simply holding it in your hand will freeze your skin, but it will feel like it is burning, not freezing. It was the most terrible moment of my life!" Fear sat heavy in his widened eyes. "The cold power of the Storm Pearl spread all over my body. Each strand of my hair was frozen to solid ice, and it felt like hundreds of blades cutting me to pieces from the inside out."

The Storm Pearl was like a demon that had been imprisoned for ages finally being unleashed. The Pearl absorbed the raw power of the person who held it; but it also released a surge of power to gain control over them.

Gia was immediately overwhelmed by the Storm Pearl. Like Truong, his eyes froze and his whole body trembled; his skin frosted over in patterns like snowflakes. His blood turned to ice, creating scars on his forehead where his veins froze.

Fortunately, Phong was standing next to him. The young man reacted quickly: he hit Gia, and the Pearl fell out of his mouth. The hit had saved his life.

And yet, Gia was infuriated even recounting the tale; he smashed his fist onto the table, which broke into pieces. Cups fell to the ground, shattering on impact, and Dong Tu flinched. Gia looked colder, crueler, and even more powerful as he told the old story, trembling all the while.

Gia returned to the story. He had collapsed to the ground, convulsing in fits and writhing in pain. Phong and Ivy had used their chi to keep him warm. Ivy knew that if Phong failed, she would have to try the Storm Pearl. Terror turned her almost as cold as the Pearl, and she couldn't stop the frightened tears that escaped at the thought.

Thanh Nhan shook her head in disappointment. It was Phong's turn.

Phong reluctantly put the Pearl in his mouth.

The Storm Pearl itself was black at its center, as if there were a small, swirling storm inside. Phong, too, started to freeze like Truong and Gia, his color fading, his irises turning silver. Snow flurried out into the air, enveloping him like clothes. Gusts of wind roared loudly, and everyone in the main hall watched nervously as a twisting winter storm blew to life around Phong.

And then a black stain began to spread from the center of the vortex, spreading like a splash of ink in a glass of water: Phong's body had begun to put off a blistering wave of heat to combat the ice of the Pearl, and where the heat radiated, the snow blackened. The black snow quickly overwhelmed the vortex created by the Storm Pearl, and soon after, the wind slowly died down. Phong breathed deeply, his body returning to normal. The snow on his skin melted into water and dripped onto the ground.

When the scene finally settled, all that was left of the swirling storm were several black snowflakes floating off of Phong's body in an invisible wind. Gia and Ivy stood, shocked, unable to believe their eyes.

"Just as I had hoped," Thanh Nhan said confidently. "This child has absorbed Solar Radiance power. His body generates enough heat to withstand the cold of the Storm Pearl!"

"Wait!" Dong Tu interrupted Gia's flashback. "If Obsidian's real name is Phong...and if when he was a child he absorbed the Solar Radiance power...then Obsidian and Bach Duong, they're...they're..."

Gia nodded. It was all becoming clear: every time she looked at Bach Duong, something in him reminded her of Obsidian.

"That's right," Gia affirmed. "But that dandy Bach Duong doesn't know anything. He just keeps searching for Phong." He smirked. "Phong was seven years old when he came to the Poison Legion. He was old enough to remember who he was before, so whenever he's pursued by Bach Duong, he never fights back. He could never hurt his brother."

Dong Tu understood then. That night at the funeral, when Obsidian had gotten shot, it was because he had no choice. He'd been trying to save Dong Tu—and he'd refused to harm his half-brother, Bach Duong.

"That's terrible," Dong Tu gasped. "Bach Duong has no idea he almost killed his lost brother. If he had known, that would be terrible...I can't imagine the way his handsome face would look if he found out."

"Handsome face? Have you seen Phong?" Gia protested.

Gia, Dong Tu noticed, was full of contradictions.

Although he would never admit he was less powerful than Phong, he would also never let anyone be better than Phong. It seemed he wanted to compete with Phong on the smallest things, but only with Phong and no one else. Dong Tu frowned. The sibling rivalry between Gia and Phong was obvious...but he also idolized him. It was very strange.

"But wait a minute!" Gia exclaimed, suddenly remembering his original intent. "I didn't keep you here to tell you bedtime stories, after all!"

In the past, Phong had been better than Gia at everything. Phong had absorbed the Storm Pearl, successfully cultivated the Storm Strike, and been appointed the North King of Poison. Whatever Gia had wanted, Phong had seemed to get. Gia smiled to himself. This time, *he* would have the thing that Phong wanted: Dong Tu.

Gia began to rip off Dong Tu's clothes, explaining exactly why he was so excited about her presence as he did. But he had not thought very far ahead; as he tore her shirt, Dong Tu was able to free herself from the petals and fabric pinning her to the wall. She tried to kick him in the balls, taking off running out of the room. Gia dodged her attack, following, and as soon as he was close enough he caught hold of her and jerked her back.

CHAPTER 9

Hoa Hon Palace

Phong was wounded, cranky, and running a nasty fever, and the ruckus from Gia's fighting and smashing furniture had woken him from his fitful sleep. He'd known that Dong Tu had sought him out, but he had politely asked Lady Ivy to send her away. Even though he'd known it would be best in the long run, the guilt had been eating him up, and after Dong Tu had left, he had been interrogated by Ivy about their kiss. The whole mess had made him so uncomfortable that he couldn't truly go back to sleep afterward, no matter how hard he tried.

When he was brought to the Poison Legion at seven years old, Bach Phong had known there was no way out. His normal life was over. Even when he'd discovered Bach Duong was his elder brother, he had forced himself to ignore it, and therefore spent his life running from him. The thought of a romantic relationship had not crossed his mind for a long time...until he met Dong Tu. He had kissed her, randomly, without any idea why. Now he was dealing with the consequences, stuck in the middle of a situation he did not know how to handle.

Mentally, he felt like his thoughts were tangled bits of yarn and he couldn't find his way around them. The wound on his neck stung terribly, he had a high fever, his head ached, and his throat felt hot and dry. In short, he was already miserable.

To make matters worse, Hoa Hon Palace was always unbearably hot and stuffy. Its fumes felt unusually suffocating.

What is all that banging and crashing?

Obsidian had decided the most reasonable thing to do was to go to Gia's room and find out what it was. When he kicked the door open to see Dong Tu struggling in Gia's grasp, he lost it. Murderous fury twisted Obsidian's face into a scowl and gleamed coldly in his eyes.

"She belongs to me!" Obsidian snarled, his voice sharp with anger.

"Just in time for the show!" Gia greeted Obsidian with a smile and drew his favorite weapons from their place on the wall. They were a pair of sai: long, cruelly sharp daggers with quillons that curved up along the sides of each dagger from the hilt, sharpened into lethal points.

Obsidian was bare-chested beneath his robe, but when he saw Dong Tu's clothes hanging from her body like rags, he didn't hesitate to wrap her in it instead; suddenly his fever didn't seem so important.

Obsidian had been mentally prepared to fight Gia and release his anger, but when he put his robe on Dong Tu, he saw her eyes were wet from crying. *This girl has suffered so much to meet me here*, Obsidian thought. He suddenly lost all interest in fighting.

But yet in front of Gia, he could never comfort her or tell her, *I'm sorry, I shouldn't have avoided you.* There was no way he would humiliate himself in such a vulnerable and tacky way in front of Gia!

"Don't you dare use chi in here!" Gia warned him. Gia spun his pair of sai in his hands like two pinwheels. The weapons glinted in the candlelight, swishing intimidatingly through the air.

Obsidian used his bare hands.

Two young men, shirtless in the bamboo room, fought over an ordinary girl.

Gia's sharp weapons spun mercilessly, but when he rushed in, Obsidian easily caught hold of one right away. He grasped the tip of the sai and held it tight. Gia bit his lip, using all his strength to resist; veins stuck out prominently on his head from the effort. He was putting up quite a fight, and while Obsidian pushed on one tip of the sai, the two others scratched his arms. The weapon left scratch marks exactly like the ones Dong Tu had seen on Obsidian's body.

Even though Obsidian was in a fierce fight, Dong Tu heaved a sigh of relief. *So those scratches weren't caused in bed by Lady Ivy's nails,* she rejoiced silently.

Gia knew he was losing. He released the sai, curled his hand into a fist, and landed a punch right on his opponent's neck––directly on his wound. Obsidian tried to cry out in pain, but it came out choked. *Gia's playing dirty again,* he realized, unsurprised. It was one of Gia's habits. *Fine! All bets are off!*

Gia caught his weapons and charged for a second time. This time, Obsidian was ready. He used his chi to keep the sai in the air. The energy from his hand turned into freezing air, causing the moisture in the room to form frozen crystals. The icy air coalesced around Gia's hand, causing him to hiss and drop the weapon. The sai clattered to the ground.

"Don't you dare break—" Even before Gia finished his sentence, the weapon cracked from the inside, shattering into three pieces.

"Not again! That's my *favorite* weapon!" Gia's rage made him choke with anger, unable to continue.

Obsidian paid no attention to Gia. He wrapped his arm around Dong Tu and led her back to his room.

The sun had long since set, and the thrilling scene that Anole and Switch had been waiting for was finally happening: Obsidian and Dong Tu were staying together in the same room!

The night birds sang their lullabies outside the window. Since Obsidian had so boldly claimed Dong Tu as his woman and Gia was still prowling around outside, the safest place for Dong Tu in Hoa Hon Palace at the moment was Obsidian's room. One man, one woman, one room, and one very vivid kissing incident still fresh on Obsidian's mind. This scene was too perfect.

It was even more perfect because the two talkative wanderers, Anole and Switch, were still lost somewhere in Hoa Hon. Neither could spy on the two of them–they were completely alone!

Since Dong Tu's clothes had been torn to shreds, Obsidian rummaged through his wardrobe and brought out a nightshirt for her.

"I'm sorry, but this is the smallest I can find," he concluded, after flipping his wardrobe upside down. Obsidian's smallest clothes were still far too baggy for her.

"You're so tiny," he teased. "Wearing a big shirt makes you look even smaller. I can't see you underneath all that fabric! From a distance, it looks like the shirt is walking by itself."

Dong Tu wrinkled her nose. "You're being rude. Don't talk about my body like that!"

"Sorry," Obsidian apologized, with a grin that brought his boyish dimples out in his cheeks. Obsidian always seemed kind and gentle when he was around Dong Tu. He'd even attempted a joke! It hadn't a good one, but even so, he had tried.

He was also thoughtful. When Dong Tu's stomach grumbled, he ordered his servant to bring her dinner. He didn't eat, as he still hadn't fully recovered from his neck injury and didn't have an appetite. He simply sat quietly and watched her with a soft smile and adoring eyes.

When she finished her last bite, Dong Tu looked up and caught Obsidian's expression. Her cheeks flushed and she lowered her head, unable to meet his eyes. She picked at the table's surface nervously. *That day I came back from the dead,* she thought, *I heard everyone gossiping about how Obsidian kissed me. Could they have told the truth?*

After seeing that look in his eyes, Dong Tu could not help but hope.

She still didn't know what to make of him. They had just met, and their situation was so complicated. Switch, Anole, and Leatherback had teased them both a little too much. *But I'm just an ordinary girl; I'm nothing compared to the wonderful beauty of Lady Ivy. I bet she's a perfect martial artist, too.*

Yet, for some inexplicable reason, Obsidian cared for Dong Tu.

"Oh, no..." Obsidian brushed his fingers over a red spot Ivy's poisoned handkerchief had left on Dong Tu's cheekbone. He dug out the antidote and dotted some on the spot, apologizing. "Ivy is cruel. I'm sorry she caused you pain, Dong Tu."

Dong Tu was silent for a moment, not sure how to respond; she couldn't wrap her mind around the odd relationship Obsidian and Ivy seemed to have.

"Is Lady Ivy your girlfriend?" she asked finally.

"No; we grew up together. She's more like a younger sister. Why do you ask?" Obsidian replied. Dong Tu's face was so red that he couldn't tell which spots were irritated by the poison and which were her natural color.

It was getting awkward, and Dong Tu could not keep her head bowed anymore. She had to raise her face for Obsidian to apply the medicine. When she looked up and met his eyes, her limbs seemed to stop working, and she could feel her face turn even redder. Though she tried to glance to the side, pretending to look at the lanterns or the dried flower basket hanging from the ceiling, eventually she couldn't help but look into his deep eyes. *He might be cold and thorny on the outside*, she thought, *but right now, in front of me, he is gentle and kind.*

Obsidian looked much more worn down than the last time they had met. His face had a sickly green tint to it, his jaw and neck were covered in stubble, and his hair was shaggy. But he was still the same Obsidian with those long lashes, gentle eyes, and wide shoulders. *And*, she realized, *his skin still has that fresh-cut grass smell. It's so delightful! I wonder if he tastes like he smells...?*

Dong Tu felt so odd. She had grown up with Bao Thuong; it wasn't as if her father's dojo was strictly for females. She had met many other extraordinarily good-looking men in her life, even Obsidian's brother, Bach Duong. If you compared the two, Bach Duong was much more striking and well-dressed. But only Obsidian had made her feel so safe and sound; comfortable, yet excited.

He kept dabbing the medicine on her face, both lost in their thoughts. Both of them had things to say–and both were too shy to be the first to speak.

"Thank you." Dong Tu finally broke the silence. "How's the wound on your throat?" She had noticed that his voice was hoarse, and was worried that the arrow wound had damaged his vocal cords.

"Oh, that? It's doing fine. My voice is so bad because Ivy got a sore throat while taking care of my injuries, and she gave it to me," Obsidian explained. "It's nothing to worry about."

"Are you sure? It's bleeding," Dong Tu pointed out.

Unsurprisingly, when Obsidian and Gia had fought, Gia's punch had reopened his neck wound. Somehow he hadn't noticed it until Dong Tu mentioned it—but the moment she did, it began to hurt.

"Dong Tu, would you help me change my bandage?" Obsidian requested. "It's in a place I can't see myself."

Dong Tu nodded and carefully unwrapped his bandage. Gia had known the wound was a weak spot for Obsidian, and his punch had done more damage than she had thought. She was afraid of hurting Obsidian while she applied the medicine, so she only barely touched his skin. He smiled.

"It is okay. I'm used to it, Dong Tu. Just apply it as you would to anyone else."

"But doesn't it hurt?"

"No."

"Not even when you got shot?"

"Uh...no!"

Of course he couldn't admit that the arrow had been extremely painful. When he'd gotten shot, and the whole way back to Hoa Hon Palace, he had thought he was going to die. He had felt every minute of the pain and blood loss. He had drained all his chi for the Soul Streak and the Storm Strike, exhausting his body so thoroughly he'd almost stopped breathing. Obsidian remembered falling into a trance, hearing nothing but the sound of his heart pounding in his chest.

When he finally reached the steps of Hoa Hon Palace, he had been on the brink of collapse. His mind reeled, his whole body had frozen, and he had lost consciousness right there at the gate. During his coma, he'd replayed the memory of taking Dong Tu out of the coffin, of their strange kiss...

When he woke up, sweaty, several days later, he realized he had talked during his coma. Obsidian fuzzily saw Ivy and Samsara looking down at him with concerned faces.

"Who on earth is Dong Tu?"

"What sect does this Master Dong Tu lead?"

Obsidian had just opened his eyes, but he was immediately bombarded with questions from Ivy and Samsara, the leader of the Poison Legion. They wanted to know who had been able to injure Obsidian and why he had called out her name while he was unconscious. Who was this Dong Tu? Where did Master Dong Tu come from? How powerful was she? Why had she hurt Obsidian, and what was she planning to do against the Poison Legion and the Valley of Life and Death?

Obsidian didn't know where to even begin to explain the tangled series of events.

Back in the present, Dong Tu was right beside him, bandaging the wound on his neck. Her small hand brushed his skin, and her cute, innocent face was only inches from his own.

Dong Tu was incredibly gentle. Before they had even gotten to know each other, she had been poisoned because of him. Yet when he'd fainted, she had stayed to care for him, not asking for anything in return. No one had been that gentle with him since before he had joined the Poison Legion. Ivy was also worried about his health, but she was just a sister to him. She might have taken care of him, but she was demanding and overly possessive. She would often carelessly use him as an unwilling test subject for her new poisons. And then there was Gia, who was jealous of the Storm Pearl Obsidian had.

Only Dong Tu had cared for him.

She was cute, an average girl; not stunning, not overly fierce, but still kind. Not a damsel in distress who always needed protection or pampering, and certainly not a rude woman who enjoyed mocking and bullying others, like Ivy. Dong Tu was the type of girl that made people embrace her and beg for her affections.

When he was next to Dong Tu, Obsidian felt peace. Every fight and every injury faded into the past. The only important thing was the present, where Dong Tu was–– opposite him, bandaging his wound. He only needed to bend a little closer to touch her soft lips. *If I did that, if I kissed Dong Tu on the lips...she isn't unconscious this time,* he thought. *I bet she would kiss me back. And if I did, I would be able to touch her soft skin again, and her adorable cheeks, and her beautiful neck. And...*

"Don't lower your head like that, Obsidian–I can't tighten the bandage like that," Dong Tu said suddenly. Their faces were just a breath apart.

Obsidian blinked, sighed, and raised his head to look at the ceiling. A new pang throbbed through his chest, like an invisible hand rubbing salt on a wound. The pain shot through his heart. He needed to get his head on straight: he *couldn't* fall for this girl.

Wait a minute...there's just the two of us in this room...

A boy and a girl, together in a room, in the quiet of the night. Anything could happen.

Dong Tu was innocent. Her thoughts had not yet gone there. But Obsidian was not so innocent. His mind kept wandering back to the first day he saw her, how she had caught his eye, and how they had "kissed." Now they were spending the night in the same room. She was even wearing his clothes, which made her attractive in an awkwardly cute way. The shirt hung off of one of her shoulders, while on him it was tight. *She's just so small,* Obsidian thought, *and it makes her even cuter...and those adorable lips...*

Crap! My mind is wandering again. This is crazy! There's two of us in this one room, and I can't keep my mind off kissing her. I need another distraction.

"Dong Tu, would you like to watch fireflies?" he offered quickly. "Let's go outside. There's an observation tower here, and when the palace rotates it's very interesting to watch! You can even look out over the lake and land and see the fireflies."

Dong Tu agreed without a second thought. Obsidian's room was spacious, but with him shirtless beside her, she could hear her own heartbeats echoing from the walls. Going outside would be best for both of them.

Obsidian put his robe back on, and he led her to the Star Observatory of Hoa Hon Palace. The observatory was located in the center of the palace, and when they reached the top, Dong Tu realized that Lady Ivy, besides having a talent for lying, actually had quite good taste in architecture.

The Observatory was a big, flat space at the highest point of the island. Dark shapes of clouds floated lazily across the sky. Below them was the mysterious, slow-turning architecture of Hoa Hon Palace. It was a bright night: stars filled the sky, and on the ground, the rotation of the palace made the glimmer of lanterns below pass in the swirling smoke as if drawing light trails. The view was marvelous.

Obsidian deliberately kept distance between he and Dong Tu. They sat on the lawn, watching the stars and talking about whatever came to mind.

Since he had joined the Legion, Obsidian had been taught the art of crafting poisons and medicines by Thanh Nhan. He had a vast amount of knowledge about botany and entomology. And he was surprised to see that the Star Observatory, which was typically full of mosquitoes, currently had none.

As the night went on, they eventually became tired of sitting. Dong Tu and Obsidian lay down, continuing to watch the stars, chatting easily. Before they knew it, they had eased into sleep.

It was cool, almost chilly, outside. As the night wore on, each of them followed the warmth of the other's body, curling up together instinctively without either one realizing it.

Dong Tu woke up in Obsidian's arms; he was hugging her like a pillow, still sound asleep, holding her tightly. His robe covered them both like a blanket. Outside, the early morning temperature was still chilly, and under the robe, they kept each other warm. Obsidian was still shirtless, and the herbal scent of his skin mixed with the strong smell of early morning grass.

His breath was hot on the back of her neck. Dong Tu was a bit startled, and at first she wanted to move, but then she noticed that Obsidian was fast asleep––his breathing steady, his eyelashes unmoving, his face peaceful and happy. She smiled and allowed herself to sink back into the warmth and safety he brought her. Dong Tu wiggled closer, rubbed her head against his chest, snaked her arm around Obsidian's waist...and pretended to sleep.

After a while Obsidian woke as well. He, too, was startled at how close Dong Tu was to him. He felt like he should move, but he didn't want to trade her warmth for the cool morning mist. Under his robe it was cozy and comfortable, so he just curled up again, leaning in to kiss Dong Tu's hair.

Dong Tu could feel Obsidian's delicate kiss and knew that he had awoken. He was still holding her tightly, his arms muscular and warm, and with both of them pretending to sleep like this, who would pretend to wake up first?

CHAPTER 10

The Duel

As it turned out, it took a third person to wake them up. And, unfortunately, their wakeup call was the unusual owner of Hoa Hon Palace: Ivy.

Ivy had risen early to go jogging; she saw Phong holding Dong Tu from afar as they lay in the Star Observatory, and without a second thought, she launched five needles in their direction.

Before the needles even began to soar, a shadow from the rock *whooshed* by, using a claw to split each needle into three.

The claw belonged to Anole.

Anole and Switch had snuck around the palace all night, finally settling in the tower to sleep. When Obsidian and Dong Tu had arrived, the duo hid themselves in a corner; and while Obsidian and Dong Tu enjoyed the spectacular view of the bright stars, the two nosy eccentrics were delighted to watch the romance unfold before their eyes.

The Monstrous Duo had known that Obsidian would be able to sense their presence if they so much as moved, so they sat still all night as mosquitoes ate them alive, only making sneaky eye contact with each new *thrilling* development. They were curious and excited, wanting to see more—and were sorely disappointed when nothing especially eventful happened.

In fact, the only thing of note that happened was that they provided a splendid a feast for the mosquitoes. The pests weren't interested in Obsidian's poisonous body, and Dong Tu gestured energetically when she talked, which made her a harder target. Between those two and the unmoving pair of delicious masters, the mosquitoes chose to attack the easiest prey, and Anole and Switch had to bite their lips to keep silent until dawn. They had decided their suffering was in vain when *finally* the two "sleeping" lovebirds snuggled up to each other. Anole and Switch were delighted that their patience had paid off––but then, of course, Ivy appeared, ruining the moment.

Anole sliced the needles in thirds so as to not disturb Obsidian and Dong Tu, but the movement and chopping sounds were more than enough to pull the lovebirds out of their pretend slumber. Obsidian and Dong Tu sat up, embarrassed.

"Phong! *Why* is that tramp still here?" Ivy shouted. "I'll kill her!" She pulled out more needles and held them between her fingers in a glittering clenched fist.

"No!" Obsidian pushed Dong Tu behind his back.

"She had the gall to step into my palace! That's enough reason to kill her! She was even *cuddling* my darling Phong. I won't let her get away with it!" Ivy persisted.

"Stop it!" Obsidian still stood between the two girls.

"Well, well...your man Phong's protecting the outsider over you." Switch popped her head out of the bush, her face covered in red, swollen bumps. "Your man has a girlfriend. Dong Tu is his lover! They kissed passionately all night!"

"WE DID NOT KISS!" Obsidian and Dong Tu shouted in unison.

"That's right, they just spooned!" Anole laughed and licked his tongue seductively.

The accused lovebirds looked at each other awkwardly, unsure of what to say.

Ivy's face flushed with fury. She rushed Dong Tu, but Obsidian protected her: he caught any needles Ivy launched, and when she changed tactics and tried to use her hands, Obsidian still blocked her. Finally, with no needles left, Ivy was forced to let Obsidian subdue her. He picked her up, carried her to her room, threw her inside and locked the door.

"Let me out!" she screamed, pounding angrily on the door. "I'm going to kill that wench, I'm going to skewer her with more needles than a thorny cactus!"

The commotion throughout the palace woke Gia. He shook his head and walked out into the hallway, only to see Obsidian tossing Ivy into her room as Switch, Anole, and Dong Tu watched. From Ivy's vengeful screaming, Gia had a good guess as to what had happened.

"It's the girls' fight, why did you interfere?" Gia complained. "It's not good that you keep bullying me and Ivy like this."

"He's right. Ivy will never win with Obsidian protecting Dong Tu," Anole agreed.

"Let the two girls fight each other," Gia suggested. "If Ivy wins, Phong must give Dong Tu to me. If that girl wins—"

Before he could finish, a vase enveloped in a glowing nebula of Ivy's chi came crashing through her door and hit him on the head.

"There's no way that *pumpkin* would ever win, so don't even think about the possibility!" Ivy yelled from her room; apparently the thought had been even more infuriating than being locked in her room to begin with.

Gia kicked the door angrily.

"I said *if!*" he shouted back, rubbing his head where the vase had hit him. "Of course, Dong Tu, you'll never beat Ivy.

148

You may as well prepare to die. Even if you stick to Phong like glue, she will hunt you to the ends of the earth!"

Gia understood Ivy's personality all too well. She was aggressive and vengeful, and from childhood she'd always wanted to have "her dear Phong" all to herself. The only reason she hadn't killed Dong Tu on sight the day before was that her dear Phong had said he wasn't interested in her. Since she had found out that Obsidian not only *liked* Dong Tu but had also spent the night with her, though, there was no way she would let it go. Her nature had always been violent, and she had been raised in the way of the Poison Legion—whomever Ivy set out to kill would end up dead by her hand.

Besides, if she insisted on ending Dong Tu, Gia might even want to help. Not to mention the fact that if Ivy and Gia reported to their leader and Thanh Nhan that Obsidian was falling for an outsider, the entire Poison Legion would track Dong Tu down and kill her anyway.

In short, unless Dong Tu really did remain attached to Obsidian at all times, she would never survive, and even then, it wasn't a sure bet. Obsidian could protect Dong Tu from Gia and Ivy, but if the whole Poison Legion and Thanh Nhan joined them, they could easily overwhelm him.

"Aha! I have a great idea!" Anole snapped his fingers. "Let's have a duel!"

Only Anole would think that was a good idea.

"Hear me out! Obsidian will be the prize!" Anole declared. "If Lady Ivy wins, she gets to have her dear Phong back. If Dong Tu wins, Lady Ivy must leave Dong Tu and her dear Phong alone from now on, without reporting it to the leader of the Poison Legion."

"No!" Obsidian and Gia both raised their voices. That was ridiculous! Ever since they were children, Obsidian had only ever viewed Ivy as a sister. He absolutely could not marry her!

Gia, on the other hand, protested because he would gain nothing from the deal.

"I agree!" Ivy said, sticking her head out of the hole she'd made in the door with the vase.

"No!" Obsidian, Gia, and Dong Tu refused.

Ivy cupped a hand beside her mouth, pretending to call out, "Oh, Thanh Nhan...!"

Knowing that she would never let it go, Obsidian sighed.

"Alright! Fine," He conceded, frustrated. *I can't believe I agreed to this.*

Obsidian set the rules. Since Dong Tu had been poisoned by him, she could no longer use her chi, and as such, they could only allow pure martial arts. No powers. No poison.

Even without the use of inner power or poison, Ivy could still beat Dong Tu, and she knew it. She grinned sneakily, pinky swearing to Obsidian that she would only use martial arts. Ivy even agreed to let Obsidian, Anole, and Switch work with Dong Tu in order to prepare her for the duel; after three days, they would meet again at the Star Observatory.

After the deal was sealed, Obsidian took Dong Tu to the training room. He found books on fighting techniques and gave them to Dong Tu.

"These are a few techniques of the Poison Legion that Ivy knows the best. If you master them, you will beat Ivy."

Dong Tu trembled as she listened. She knew that Lady Ivy was much, much more experienced than her. *I'll never be able to beat her, let alone with such little time to prepare!*

"Don't worry too much!" Anole and Switch tried to comfort her. "We'll help! We can teach you a few secret techniques!" After all, they were both members of the infamous Monstrous Eighteen.

"I can help too!" Gia said from the back of the training room. Gia had a crush on Ivy. He didn't care about Dong Tu, but he could not let Ivy win and marry Phong. And with Gia on the list, Dong Tu had four martial arts masters willing to teach her.

"I guess it could be worse," she said with a rueful smile.

Switch volunteered first. She taught Dong Tu the basic art of power exchange: Capricious Heart.

"Every ordinary person has chi. You can develop it through practicing martial arts, which teaches you how to control inner power," Switch explained. "I was born with no inner power."

"Except when she can't digest her food--then she definitely has inner *and* outer power!" Anole teased her. Switch fired back a response, and the two began a squabble which delayed the teaching until they were reminded there were more important things at stake.

Switch finally returned to the subject.

Being born without chi, Switch had been unable to master that side of the martial arts for a long time. In order to substitute for her lack of power, she had learned how to capture and control others' chi and draw it into herself—hence the name.

"The first step is learning to use your hands," Switch explained, and demonstrated. Her movements became soft and smooth, as if she were made of liquid, and smoke coalesced into balls in each hand. It was beautiful to behold.

"When two people are fighting, use the power exchange technique to swap your power for your opponent's. Ivy obviously has more power than you, so all you have to do is exchange her power with yours," Switch concluded. "The only way to beat Ivy is to cheat like this!"

"Hold on, hold on," Anole interrupted. "That technique is very dangerous!"

Switch nodded. "That's true. The greatest weakness of this technique is that if your power and your opponent's power clash, you can die."

"That's not what I mean!" Anole shook his head. "If you really want to use the power swap technique, you have to focus to engage your chi beforehand! Switch, you have no inner power, but you're still able to engage your chi. But since Dong Tu kissed Obsidian, she has already been poisoned and taken Bach Duong's antidote. How can she engage her chi? There's no way she can use your method and survive."

"Damn it." Switch passed a hand over her face. "I guess you don't realize how important something is until you lose it. Goes for power as well as everything else. Ugh, she can't use her chi! She's as useless as if she were dead, except she's even more useless, because she's *not* dead!" She pulled at her hair, pieces of her old face cracking and falling to the floor.

As it turned out, more of Switch's version of martial arts were based on inner power than she had thought.

"Well, I guess I'll teach you a different technique!" Switch said, shaking her head. After thinking for a while, she remembered one rare move which did not require chi: the wind siphon technique. Switch siphoned Dong Tu's chi from her body; ordinarily, when someone was attacked with power from the outside, their internal chi would automatically fight back, resulting in internal damage. With the siphoning technique, Dong Tu's chi was nullified: if she were attacked, the outside force would pass through her body without causing any injuries.

GIAO CHI

Next came Anole's turn. He was sure that if Dong Tu used his techniques, she would definitely be able to beat Ivy. Anole's talents were his speed and his claws, his moves fast and sophisticated.

"You obviously don't have claws, so you can use darts between your fingers," he explained.

He also taught Dong Tu "lizard recites poem" and "drop the tail."

"First," Anole said, "use the darts to grab hold of the wall or the ceiling. If you master this skill, you can fight on the ceiling as easily as on the ground. You should always take advantage of every surface wherever you're fighting. Second, you can use the darts in your fingers to break things, like I did with Lady Ivy's needles. If you can figure out where the weakest parts of a weapon are, you can break it easily."

Gia taught Dong Tu a move which was only reserved for the masters of the Poison Legion: himself, Phong, and Ivy.

"This is an extremely special move called Sting of a Thousand Poisons," Gia instructed Dong Tu. "Use your pointer finger, middle finger, and pinky to aim at your opponent and hit their neck three times. The people of the Poison Legion tend to use poison with this move. Anyone who gets hit will have their chi reversed, and it will also cut off the blood flow to their head. If they don't die immediately, they certainly won't be able to stay alive for long! Since you don't have any chi or poison, using the Sting will only be enough to make Ivy choke. But at least when she attacks, you'll know what to expect," Gia explained. He'd already predicted that Ivy would win immediately.

"Sting of a Thousand Poisons uses very tender and flexible moves, like dancing," he added. "Watching you two beautiful ladies use it in your duel will be a show! Dong Tu, you should change into something sexy like what Ivy wears when you fight." His hand found its way to her waist as he spoke—and Obsidian forcefully punched a hole in the wall, staring straight at Gia. Gia let go of Dong Tu.

"I'm only teaching her techniques, nothing else..." He trailed off.

Obsidian ground his teeth, his forehead wrinkled into straight lines of anger.

From the day the deal had been struck, Obsidian had accompanied Dong Tu everywhere she went. He even set a small bed for himself at the door of her room, so no one could get in without him knowing. His protection had already been needed—like when some *mysterious* needles had launched straight at Dong Tu's back, or the food *coincidentally* smelled like poison.

Obsidian was following and watching her closely...and yet Gia still had the nerve to keep touching her.

What made him the angriest was that when he taught Dong Tu, Gia was always there to "observe." Even after Obsidian kicked him out, Gia would come back, and he wasn't the only one. Whenever Obsidian and Dong Tu were alone in the practice gym, everyone else lost no opportunity to sneak around and annoy them. Switch and Anole didn't want to miss seeing if the two took advantage of their alone time to kiss or cuddle. Even Ivy would *accidentally* stop by to see if anyone wanted to drink (poisoned) tea.

And that wasn't the worst of it.

The servants at Hoa Hon Palace usually viewed Obsidian as a cold and lonely person who would rarely visit the palace. Now he had returned with a girl–one he cared for, protected, and taught. That kind of unusual spectacle drew a crowd of watchers.

As a result, even though the gym was quite spacious and comfortable, the two felt like they were performing onstage. Each unavoidable touch that occurred while sparring didn't bring a sense of romance, only stress.

Obsidian taught Dong Tu four unique techniques. The first required the use of a staff, which was Obsidian's weapon of choice. The second required dual-wielding a pair of sai, Gia's favorite weapon. The third involved Ivy's flying needles. Dong Tu had to use needle magnets between her fingers, spreading the sharp tips out like a fan. The fourth and final technique required the use of two iron rings. Dong Tu wasn't told whose signature weapon the iron rings were.

Three days, eight techniques, and all eight moves of the high-level martial arts masters. Dong Tu practiced day and night.

———

The day finally came, and everyone arrived at the Star Observatory on time. No one was going to miss this.

For such a solemn activity, it was truly a beautiful day, unusually sunny for the misty island, with a light breeze blowing sweetly across it. Colorful butterflies rested on flowers opposite the serious faces of the participants.

Ivy dressed fashionably for the occasion. Her "armor" consisted of a combination of metallic ropes. Her hair was rolled into a bun, and sharp needles like those of a cactus were tied at her hips. Her purple-and-green skirt flowed in the wind like the wings of a butterfly. Meanwhile, Dong Tu wore only simple white clothes with a red silk belt.

The two young ladies stood opposite each other. Ivy was confident that she would win the battle and stared challengingly at Dong Tu, refusing to avert her gaze. Anole, Switch, Obsidian, and Gia waited anxiously with the audience.

Dong Tu, of course, was the most anxious of them all. The outcome of this battle seriously affected the marriage of...well, Obsidian. As she glanced through the audience,

Dong Tu could see the serious and worried face of the "prize." It stressed her even more.

Quarter one began.

Ivy drew a fan made of needles from somewhere behind her back. Her lips curved into an expression that sat somewhere between a smile and a baring of teeth. As Ivy flicked the fan open and closed, the needles flashed wickedly.

Anole waved his hand to start the battle. Right away, each girl attacked. Dong Tu used Anole's slicing technique, aiming at the central point of the needle fan with the aid of eight powerful darts. Many of Ivy's fan needles were snapped off at the middle. For Ivy, however, a broken weapon did not mean defeat. She twisted, pushing the unbroken needles into Dong Tu's hand.

Obsidian grimaced as if he felt Dong Tu's pain.

Score: Ivy: 1, Dong Tu: 0.

Quarter two.

Ivy was relentless in her attack. Each time she moved her now-broken needle fan, the needles poured out like rain. Dong Tu used the staff to block the needles, sending them ricocheting back into the audience. Fortunately, each spectator was *apparently* a super kung fu master, and easily avoided the needles without batting an eye. Some of the needles buried themselves in the food on the refreshments table that had been set up, and the snacks took on the appearance of porcupines.

The needles were strong, and Ivy could close her eyes and launch them exactly on target. Dong Tu had only practiced with the staff for less than three days. When she covered one part of her body, another was hit by the needles. Eventually the pain caused her to drop the staff and cry out.

Score: Ivy: 2, Dong Tu: 0.

Anole bit his teacup. Spitting out the piece of broken china, he whispered to himself, "Dong Tu isn't good enough to win!"

Obsidian paled. It was clear they had overestimated Dong Tu's abilities during training. To the extraordinary wanderers, three days was plenty of time to learn new skills; with Dong Tu, however, it was very much not enough. *I shouldn't have let her fight, even after teaching her myself,* he thought.

I've made a terrible mistake.

Quarter 3.

Lady Ivy folded her hands in front of her chest, turning the needles into a prickly bouquet. She spun her wrists without warning, and the needle-bouquet turned into two blades and shot out at Dong Tu.

Time seemed to slow around Dong Tu as she reached up and grabbed hold of two long rattan cords from a nearby tree. The audience watched closely: none of the techniques she had learned used a whip.

But Dong Tu had finally figured out a pattern in Ivy's techniques: they all had the advantage of distance. When Ivy attacked, Dong Tu dodged quickly and used Anole's training to scuttle up a tree. She jumped down, landing close to her opponent, and lashed the rattan cord around Ivy's hands.

The audience clapped and cheered appreciatively: it was a clever move!

Incapacitated, Ivy screamed and tore the ropes using her chi, furiously flouting the rules.

Score: Ivy: 2, Dong Tu: 1.

The fourth quarter had just begun when a servant came running up. He knelt in front of Obsidian, whispering something to him. Obsidian and Gia stood up as one.

"Stop the fight now. We must go to the Collector's Hall immediately!"

CHAPTER 11

The Collector's Hall

"What happened? Why do you have to go to the Collector's Hall?" Dong Tu asked in surprise.

Dong Tu would have thought Ivy would object to the order, suddenly being forced to stop in the middle of a fight she'd been champing at the bit for; but when she heard of the urgent news, Ivy's attitude changed surprisingly quickly.

"It's Legion business, between us and Phong. Why should *you* care?" Ivy sneered at her, and Dong Tu blinked and flushed at being put back in her place so blatantly.

Obsidian's wound was not yet healed, but due to the seriousness of what was happening, he was also going. Obsidian, Ivy, and Gia prepared their gear and dressed for the journey: Obsidian wore his usual black clothes. Ivy wore her combat dress, woven of metal threads and indigo silk. Gia was shirtless, with only a ceremonial sash around the waist of his pants. His body was his weapon and his armor.

Obsidian put Anole and Switch in charge of Dong Tu.

"Take her home," he said. "This thing with the Collector is going to be dangerous, I don't want Dong Tu anywhere near it." He wanted her safe, but he didn't say that out loud—not that he had to.

He bid Dong Tu a quiet farewell, and they looked at each other, subtly tense. They didn't want to part, but Obsidian's life was not in immediate danger anymore, and Dong Tu had been spared by Ivy. There were no excuses left for her to stay.

"Will I ever see you again?" Dong Tu's question was barely more than a whisper.

"What was that?" Obsidian asked with a frown; he hadn't heard the words.

Dong Tu didn't have the courage to repeat herself, so she remained silent and shook her head.

Finally Obsidian donned his mask, the gentleness in his eyes fading into hardness. Only the cold, deadly gaze that the Whispered World knew so well remained.

Anole, Switch, and Dong Tu left the island, but it soon became clear that the two eccentrics weren't going to follow *orders*. Obviously. They looked at each other.

"To the Collector's Hall?" Switch asked, raising her eyebrows.

"I thought you'd never ask," Anole agreed as he stretched his shoulders and rubbed his sleeves. "Wherever there's a fight, there is fun!"

That was their life motto.

Not giving Dong Tu another second to respond, Switch continued: "Your Obsidian has been seriously wounded, what if he gets more injuries during battle? Don't you want to follow your lover and see how he's doing?"

Switch had read Dong Tu's mind like an open book, and so they all set off, doing exactly as expected and not at all as they had been told.

———

Obsidian had been in the care of Hoa Hon Palace since his injury, so the mutant captured at the Collector's Hall couldn't have been him—but Bach Duong and his traveling companions didn't know that. They had followed the poor swordsman Phong to the Collector's Hall, and by the time they arrived, a massive gathering was underway.

The Collector's Hall was actually a massive estate, replete with a lake and botanical garden. The garden and all its inhabitants—birds of paradise and other exotic species— were well taken care of by their gardeners, who appeared to be gentle, artistic beings.

And who were actually a trained security force.

The scenery and architecture of the estate were magnificent. The proprietor of the Collector's Hall, Quach Tam Phuong, had once been a gangster of the Whispered World. After retiring, he constructed the hall and amassed a collection of the works of the greatest poets, authors, musicians, and artists, alongside other treasured collections, including volumes of martial arts manuscripts handed down through the centuries in the mystical, criminal circles of the Whispered World. He had studied and mastered them all.

The Collector's Hall was not only his sanctuary away from home, but also an exhibition hall to display the freaks he'd bought or captured among his priceless artwork. Quach Tam Phuong knew how to make things work for his own benefit: his one-of-a-kind collections were also a way to fill his wealthy pockets by selling viewing tickets and room rentals during his exhibition events.

Just then, Quach Tam Phuong was holding an event to show off his newly captured exhibit piece, whose name was being kept a secret. It was only announced that the mystery being was in possession of the Storm Pearl.

Money was not an issue for Bach Duong and his people. They rented rooms and bought exhibition tickets without a second thought. The swordsman Phong accompanying him was treated as a guest as well: he was given accommodation in a similarly expensive room at the south wing of the Collector's Hall.

On the way to their rooms, they came upon a large gathering of people beside the lake.

The crowd was talking and pointing at a mutant, craning their necks to get a better look. His fur-covered body was as unusual as his height—double that of a normal person.

He was accompanying a young woman who was playing with paper boats by the lake. The mutant's size and muscles were menacing, and his face was covered with rough, ugly tumors, but the young woman—a great beauty—was not intimidated.

Xuan Thu had never seen anyone so beautiful in her life. The angelic woman leaned over to adjust one of the paper boats in the water before her, and it floated off with her touch. She was made even more captivating by her elegant, white silk dress, its train draped across the ground in ceremonial fashion. The dress illuminated her face, made even more stunning as the glimmering reflections of the lake danced over her like a celestial aura.

The light glinting off the waves hit the gold flecks in her mesmerizing light-brown eyes and made them glow like golden leaves falling from trees in autumn. One could be drowned by the beauty of her eyes...or by the depths of what seemed like an endless sadness housed within them.

Even Bach Duong, who was familiar with such ethereal beauties, gasped in surprise. The poor swordsman Phong was stunned.

The young woman and the mutant were connected at the opposite ends of iron chains.

"Why is this beauty walking a beast?" Bach Duong exclaimed.

"More like the beast is walking the beauty," Xuan Thu corrected.

She was right. The gigantic mutant patiently waited for the beauty to gently fold another paper boat and put it in the lake. As the boat drifted away, she stared at it, nostalgic and sorrowful. Then the mutant pulled a chain, which no one had noticed at first, the end of which was attached to the young woman's ankle beneath her dress. They both stood up and prepared to leave.

"Hold on!" Bach Duong dashed in front of the two. "May I ask why this beauty is being chained?"

"Who are you? What business is this of yours?" The mutant gestured to Bach Duong with a jerk of his jaw.

Bach Duong announced his name.

The deformed master introduced himself as Big Bear, one of the Monstrous Eighteen, infamous for his height and intimidating size and highly feared in combat. Big Bear worked as a henchman for the Collector.

"And the lady is...?"

Hearing Bach Duong's uneasy concern, the chained beauty, previously oblivious to the conversation, turned her attention to them.

"My family name is Dao. I am Dao Que Chi."

Whispers rushed through the entire crowd. It wasn't a name they knew.

"Who is Miss Dao?" Thien Thien asked, and Xuan Thu shrugged her shoulders. How was she supposed to know? Thien Thien moved closer to Xuan Thu, leaning his head to get a better view of Dao Que Chi. Xuan Thu noticed Thien Thien's ears were pierced.

All the pieces clicked together. Thien Thien's strange, delicate build, the exceedingly childlike behavior, far beyond average for someone his age, the odd femininity—Thien Thien was not a eunuch, but a girl! But who was she, then?

There were so many mysterious women.

Bach Duong continued to question Big Bear as Xuan Thu had her revelation, wanting to know why Dao Que Chi was in chains.

"If you really want to know, wait 'til exhibition day! She is our prisoner. Taking her out to see the flowers was a special allowance of the Collector!"

Angered by his response, Bach Duong replied, "This is insane, how could you imprison people without any clear cause?"

Someone from the crowd spoke. "Please calm down, Bach Duong!"

The spectators closest to the approaching voice cleared the way as the Collector, Quach Tam Phuong himself, emerged. The onlookers fell silent in a wide ripple.

Quach Tam Phuong was over sixty, but still strong and healthy. He wore a simple yet elegant silk shirt that would have been more at home on a scholar, but when he moved, one could see the neck tattoos leftover from his golden days spent running the world's dark underbelly.

"The Collector's Hall, from its establishment to now, has only captured notorious criminals. Everyone, please, do not be fooled by this villain's appearance. Who is Dao Que Chi? Please be patient. In three days, when I open her exhibit, I will explain. Now, please return to your rooms!"

"The Collector has spoken!" An elderly man with a long beard announced from the crowd. Stepping forward, Ky Nguyen, head of a well-respected local dojo, continued. "As he said, the Collector's Hall does not arrest people without cause. Young master Bach, you should go. You are inexperienced and have no idea how wicked the Whispered World is. Do not make a mistake and be fooled by her captivating beauty."

Confused whispers could be heard throughout the crowd. The Collector's Hall was indeed reputable, and didn't indiscriminately persecute...but Dao Que Chi's innocent, enchanting beauty inspired an odd kind of devotion in those who looked upon her.

Bach Duong felt like *someone* should be chivalrous and come to the girl's defense, as she seemed reluctant to speak up for herself, but the Collector had insinuated that Bach had come to her defense because of her beauty rather than because it was right; he didn't want to make himself look worse.

Dao Que Chi spoke to support him. "I appreciate your effort, young master. I am deeply grateful. But I'm just an ordinary girl. Please do not let my troubles upset you."

She then turned her attention back to one of the floating boats. Bach Duong's heart ached like it was being stabbed by a hundred knives, and it pained him to back down, but he remained silent.

As the crowd began to disperse and go to their rooms, Bach Duong thought to himself, *Dao Que Chi, you beauty, who are you? How could a beautiful girl like you belong to the Whispered World?*

The show ended, the beauty was led back to her cage, and the crowd dissolved.

"What a beautiful girl. Is she for sale?" asked a familiar voice from the remaining spectators. Xuan Thu looked up and discovered an acquaintance: it was none other than her almost-brother-in-law, the magistrate's coddled son, Vinh Phuc. He was accompanied by his master Duong Kien Minh. After the incident with Dong Tu, he'd cried and whined like a child, so his master had decided to lead him into the Whispered World to expand his knowledge and experience.

———

Bach Duong had two reasons for coming to the Collector's estate. First, to find the master of the poor swordsman Phong, Myo Pic; and second, to see whether the exhibit who bore the Storm Pearl was the King of Poison or not.

Finding Myo Pic was the easy part. He just needed to go to the north wing of the estate, where the cheap accommodations stood. There he found an old, scrawny, dirty man gazing at something on the ground.

"Master!" Phong exclaimed excitedly.

Myo Pic looked up in surprise without focusing directly on Bach Duong.

"Who's that?" His eyes were crusted with dried mucus, and it looked like his vision had drastically deteriorated. Contrary to Phong's youthful aura, Myo Pic was ancient; his posture was crooked, and he didn't seem to resemble a man of justice. Even more disappointing, Myo Pic had lost his arm—the very arm where the braided rope-shaped scar would have been.

"My name is Bach Duong. I was fortunate enough to meet Phong, your student, during my travels. Phong is the same age as my lost brother. I felt something familiar about him from the first moment we met. Do you know anything of Phong's past, Master Myo Pic?"

"Ah..." Myo Pic looked up at Bach Duong through his blurred vision: he couldn't find anything in common between his disciple and Bach Duong, and even if he'd had perfect vision, he suspected he still wouldn't have been able to spot it.

"Phong has a pitiful past."

Phong's full name was Luc Can Phong. Of course, his last name, Luc, and middle name, Can, had been given by Myo Pic. The old man started to tell the rest of the story and stopped himself: he was hoping Bach Duong would invite him for a drink in exchange for more information.

After drinking up half a jug of wine in the estate's wine bar, he began.

Myo Pic was a wanderer in the Whispered World, and jobless. He'd had a glorious past, but he had become depressed. His eyesight had deteriorated, and he ended up just roaming here and there, taking any job he could do. They had mostly involved hard labor. He got involved in gambling and earned enough to feed himself, but the hobby quickly became an addiction.

One night, after gambling away everything in his pockets, drunk and starved, he'd entered a small restaurant on the side of the road begging for food. The restaurant owners, a middle-aged couple, chased him away with a broom at first. Realizing that he was nearly blind and barely holding himself together—cursing himself, cursing his pitiful life—they took pity on him. He was given leftover food and allowed to stay inside the stable overnight.

Myo Pic had been given shelter from the rain and food to fill his stomach; that was all he could ask for. He happily snuggled into the hay and fell asleep.

Unfortunately, his sleep did not last long. Awakened by a scream and commotion coming from the restaurant, Myo Pic rushed out to see what was happening.

Hurrying through the back kitchen and into the restaurant, Myo Pic froze. A gangster was standing next to a table and chairs that had been knocked over, a boy beside him. The gangster looked like he was about forty years old, with a dreadful beard on his face, fat lips, and unkempt hair covering his eyes. He was dressed in black, and secured to his clothing, prominently displayed, were barbed iron rings that functioned as weapons with which to sever limbs or slice through an entire body. The child he dragged along by the wrist was about five years old, and he wept in pain. The poor owner was trying to calm the gangster down, but it only made him angrier, and he kicked the owner in the stomach.

The kick slammed the man against a wall, his head splitting with the force, and he died within seconds. His frightened wife threw down her tray and ran; the gangster didn't chase her. The smug, relaxed look on his face was enough to know that within seconds the woman's pitiful life would be over. The gangster removed the rings from their place on his chest, and, with a devilish smirk, launched them into the air.

The woman had no chance of escape and the mysterious man showed no mercy. The rings sped through the air, passed her, and then curled right back around the way they'd come like boomerangs, splitting her body in half. She didn't even have time to scream.

The gangster patted the boy's shoulder. "Phong, gather the Rings of Thorns for me!"

The boy fearfully approached the body of the dead woman and carefully lifted the rings, heavy and stained with blood. Then, suddenly, he threw them on the ground and ran into the kitchen.

"You want to run again?" The man laughed and ambled along after the boy.

Although Myo Pic's eyes were bad, he was still plenty strong enough to fight, and he wasn't going to let this child be taken. He stepped out from the shadows where he had watched the massacre and stormed after the gangster to stop him, drawing his whip. The gangster noticed Myo Pic coming after him and picked up the rings, and before he'd even fully turned to face his unexpected foe, the rings were ripping into the air behind him towards Myo Pic. It was his whip against the stranger's rings.

The rings flew past Myo Pic in the same way and boomeranged back to bring him down with lightning speed. The rapid gracefulness with which Myo Pic unleashed his whip was matched by its ability to snake through the air, as if consciously reacting to him. Every time the whip knocked the rings off their trajectory they kept returning, shredding off pieces of the whip as it attempted to deflect or wrap around them. Both of the weapons' abilities seemed equally matched. At one point, Myo Pic even had the advantage.

Seeing that, and annoyed that the fight had lasted so long, the gangster smirked again, closed his eyes as if falling into deep meditation, and began to gather his chi. A strange wind appeared out of nowhere. Within seconds, the dirt floor became a swirling dust ball; heavy currents blew across the giant fireplace, knocking the huge cooking kettle around like a bell in the wind; the restaurant door flung open with a crackling force followed by still more gusts, and the air around the gangster blew with the intensity of a hurricane, threatening to bring the whole building down.

"It was the Storm Strike!" Myo Pic whispered dramatically to those listening to his story.

"It can't be! One must bear the Storm Pearl to use the Storm Strike. If someone was able to swallow the Pearl twenty years ago, how could the Whispered World not know?" Bach Duong asked.

"You are mistaken!" Myo Pic corrected. "Anyone can learn the Storm Strike, but its true potential can only be unleashed when used by one who bears the Storm Pearl. The Pearl only enhances the technique and force to maximize the move! Indeed, even without the Pearl in one's body, the mastered technique is still powerfully effective."

Myo Pic had rushed to attack the gangster, but the storm was too much. His whip slashed through the winds, only to be caught up and blown about at random. The rings swirled, targeted their victim, flew past the whip—and Myo Pic yelled in excruciating pain as his freshly-severed arm fell to the ground.

The gangster had been about to finish him with one last move, but suddenly he heard a shrill ringing in the storm, as if thousands of distant bronze bells were tolling. He covered his ears, then rushed into the kitchen to look for the boy.

"The boy was clever. He hid in the rice pot so the gangster could not find him," Myo Pic explained. The poor swordmaster had used his own power to stop the bleeding, and then limped into the kitchen. Although on the verge of collapse from loss of blood, he could hear muffled sounds coming from a corner of the kitchen. He flicked open the lid of the large pot and saw the boy sobbing and trembling inside.

"That was Luc Can Phong," Myo Pic finished. "I don't know who he was before. His brain blocked out his memories, and he could only say one word: Phong. I felt sorry for him, so I took him in. After a few months, most of Phong's memory returned, but he remembers nothing of the tragic event itself."

Bach Duong let out a sigh.

"So that's what happened. About the gangster...who was he?"

Myo Pic had asked around about the deadly gangster with the unusual scars. He'd eventually found out his name was Ngu Long, the Sea Dragon.

"He can dash on the surface of the water like walking on flat land, and dive into water without causing ripples! His iconic weapons are those two spiky iron rings. His body is covered in black rope-like scars."

"Even on his wrist?" Bach Duong demanded eagerly. It had to be the braid that Bach Duong had seen on the wrist of the man who'd dragged his younger brother, Bach Phong, into the lake. "So the child is really my brother!"

That child *had to be* Luc Can Phong. The poor swordmaster grinned brightly and nodded.

Shock shot straight through Luc Can Phong when he realized he'd found his blood brother, his family. Bach Duong and Luc Can Phong looked at each other, speechless, eyes glazing over in tears.

One of the seven women, Friday, squinted her eyes and studied Luc Can Phong carefully.

"It would be hard to believe you two are blood brothers. Appearance-wise, even Obsidian is more like Bach Duong than Luc Can Phong."

Friday was Bach Duong's stylist, and she knew the most about his character. At first glance, the styles and auras of Bach Duong and Obsidian were vastly different, but she knew Bach Duong well enough that their similarities hadn't escaped her gaze.

"Ha ha ha, what a really nice joke, Friday." Bach Duong burst into laughter. "Am I really evil like the King of Poison?" He pretended to be cold-faced, then put on an annoyed face to mock Obsidian. His facial expressions made the girls whisper at each other.

"Now that Friday mentions it...you really do look like Obsidian."

"Who is Obsidian?" Thien Thien asked.

"Obsidian is our nemesis. Bach Duong is on a quest to kill him and bring the Storm Pearl to Grandma Pink, the Elderess." Iron Sky, the leader of the seven women, explained.

"But every time we meet, he doesn't fight, he runs! It's so frustrating!" another girl, Thursday, commented. "Maybe he knows he's no match for Bach?"

"Obsidian...what a wicked name. He must be an ugly old villain," Thien Thien muttered. He *couldn't* be good for the country.

"Not at all! He's young and handsome!" Xuan Thu said with a mysterious smile. "He seemed cold and weird, but... attractive."

"Of course, there's no way he could be as attractive and good-looking as our young master," Iron Sky hurriedly flattered at Bach Duong's frown.

"Oh, I don't know. That guy just lacked a style advisor like me. He dressed all eerie in black, and everywhere he went black snow followed. But his face was handsome!" Friday emphasized her role in giving style advice: even a handsome man like Bach Duong would have looked terrible, roaming the Whispered World while wearing an ugly mask and evil-looking outfit like the King of Poison.

"You're right," Xuan Thu said, recalling that night when he'd brought her sister back; she could clearly picture Obsidian dressed entirely in black, walking slowly into the hall amidst flurries of black snow, a white mourning band draped over his shoulders—but without the slightest hint of emotion on his face. "Obsidian looks miserable, but I think it's just because he's of the Whispered World. I think he may actually be quite young."

Obsidian's life, besides some rare happy moments with Dong Tu, was full of nightmares; but Bach Duong had been born with a silver spoon in his mouth and had been adored by General Bach all his life. Even though he was older than Obsidian, due to the lack of hardship, he looked younger.

Despite being praised for his youthful looks, Bach Duong was displeased by the girls' comparisons, and a bit worried. His effervescent joy had begun to fizzle out.

"Master Myo Pic, I thank you for taking care of my little brother for so many years. The Bach family will not forget you, and will repay you in a timely manner for your guardianship. Ngu Long is the Bach family's nemesis. Do you know where to find him?" he asked, turning to Luc Can Phong and Myo Pic.

"There's no need to search! Ngu Long is here! You can go and ask him yourself."

CHAPTER 12

The Showdown

Myo Pic pulled a piece of worn paper from his pocket; it was an advertisement for an event at the Collector's Hall. He skimmed to the bottom of the page, pointing a dirty fingernail at the fine print.

"...and the Abhorrent Apothecarist of the Valley of Life and Death."

"The Valley of Life and Death? That place is also connected to the Poison Legion!" Bach Duong said with a frown.

"The Sea Dragon, as rumor has it, withdrew from the world to become an apothecarist for them," Myo Pic explained.

That was what had driven Myo Pic to spare no expense in coming all the way to the Collector's Hall. The debt of his severed arm had to be paid. Aside from the apparent eccentric master that the Collector had just captured, who was rumored to have the Storm Pearl inside them, he would have his chance at Ngu Long of the Valley of Life and Death!

As for Bach Duong, if it was true that Ngu Long was the one who'd kidnapped Bach Phong and killed his mother, he could now face his nemesis, have his revenge, and find out whether Luc Can Phong was indeed his half brother. Their trip to the Collector's Hall wouldn't be in vain.

The day of the exhibition finally arrived.

That night the Collector's Hall held a lavish party. Servants of the estate sounded long drumrolls to welcome the arriving guests. Groups of martial artists in colorful costumes gracefully floated about in their dances while leading the guests into the auditorium. The large auditorium was so packed that many of the guests had to stand, and some of them even made their way up into the ceiling beams to sit and watch from on high. Despite the crowd, the Collector made no compromise on pomp and circumstance, with the Hall's large columns and plaster ceiling decorated with paper flowers filled with confetti and waiting to burst at just the right moment.

The arriving parties were served. The Collector, Quach Tam Phuong, delivered the opening speech, droning on until everyone was irritated by his endless self-aggrandizing. Only then did Quach Tam Phuong allow for his new *pieces* to be led out by an attendant.

According to the advertisement, three of the wandering freaks would be presented: Ngu Long the Sea Dragon, the nymph Dao Que Chi, whom they'd met on the bank of the lake, and the mysterious creature who was said to have the Storm Pearl in their body. All three were more or less related to the Storm Pearl, the Storm Strike, and its legendary power, the Storm Power. As the least valuable acquisition, Ngu Long was brought out to whet the crowd's curiosity.

Big Bear held the curtain aside as he stepped out. He dragged along another long chain, and the end of this chain was shackled to the neck of an unusually short man. Both of his legs had been amputated from the knees down, his face was marked with numerous protruding scars, and one eyeball was streaked with thick scar tissue. The sight startled Myo Pic.

"He used to be so powerful! Who could have done this to him?!"

Bach Duong was just as surprised. Could this truly be the same Ngu Long who had kidnapped Bach Phong?

"This warrior is Ngu Long the Sea Dragon, Abhorrent Apothecarist of the Valley of Life and Death!" Quach Tam Phuong announced. "The Valley has never been involved in matters of the Whispered World. However, this man is a master of the Storm Strike!"

The Collector pulled out his sword and charged at the disabled man. The latter, still shackled at the neck by iron chains, relentlessly fought back. Wind blew eerily into the auditorium as he fought.

"Is that all?" The crowd jeered. The Sea Dragon was chained by the neck and easily defeated by Big Bear and Quach Tam Phuong. What a letdown!

Bach Duong was about to offer up an explanation about how the force of the Strike had been a thousand times more powerful when he'd seen Obsidian harness it, but he stopped himself. He just wanted to know if Ngu Long really was the one who'd kidnapped Bach Phong.

"Lord Quach! Is it really true that this is Ngu Long of the Valley of Life and Death?" Duong Kien Minh, Vinh Phuc's master, asked from the crowd. "Although they are two separate entities, the Valley and the Poison Legion are technically one evil cult. Since you have captured the Valley's people, will the Poison Legion let it be, or will they come seeking revenge for this injustice? Followers of the Legion and the Valley are all extraordinarily powerful, but this mutant is both crippled and lame, unlike what was previously known."

Myo Pic walked up to the stage.

"Nearly twenty years ago, I fought Ngu Long. If this is really Ngu Long, I would have immediately recognized him! The Sea Dragon had a black braid scar on his wrist that day." Myo Pic said, pointing at the criminal's arm indignantly.

"Is it this mark?!" The Collector exclaimed theatrically, grabbing Ngu Long's wrist and lifting it. It was exactly that mark: a black braided scar in the shape of a rope. Although he had only caught a glimpse of it, Bach Duong's memory of it remained clear. It was the exact hand that grabbed Bach Phong and dragged him into the lake. Bach Duong stood up in shock.

"You barbarian! I'll kill you!" The black mark had apparently caused a strong reaction in another spectator. With a loud cry, the person jumped over the crowd, stepping on the heads of those present as she propelled herself onto the stage.

She was a woman of considerable age. Dressed simply, she might have been a beauty in the past, but her looks had faded with time. Sword drawn, the lady exclaimed, "You were the one who killed my son! I've been tracking *that* scar to find you for years, and here you are at last!" The woman swung her sword swiftly; the only thing Ngu Long could do was raise his hands to block the strike.

But Quach Tam Phuong jumped between them and blocked her, shielding Ngu Long.

"May I ask who you are, and why you are attacking my exhibit?"

The woman did not state her name, but charged forward and continued to slash at her target. Each move was clearly fueled by a rage left to fester and boil for decades, now pouring out of her in furious waves.

"Could this be—Dianthus?!" Bach Duong called out.

"Is that really Bach Phong's mother?" Xuan Thu asked, also startled.

Thien Thien was just as baffled by the situation and could only stare with wide eyes.

Guessing the woman was Dianthus, Bach Phong's mother, Bach Duong jumped to the stage with a few sword strikes, with Myo Pic following suit. Nearly twenty others rushed to the stage with grievances of their own: Ngu Long had made himself quite a few enemies.

Each one wanted to kill Ngu Long. The scene was so chaotic that instead of dragging out Dao Que Chi and the mysterious mutant who allegedly bore the Storm Pearl in their body that night, the event was postponed to the next day and the crowd was dismissed.

———

Xuan Thu was sleeping later that night when she heard a knock on the door. She stumbled out of bed and, upon opening the door, she found Thien Thien waiting there, a serious look on her face.

"I have something to ask you!"

Thien Thien dragged Xuan Thu out into the courtyard near the kitchen where no one would be passing by at that hour.

"You seem to know a lot about Sir Bach Duong! How close are the two of you, that he's taking you everywhere with him? And sometimes even looks at you with such adoration?" Thien Thien demanded impatiently.

Xuan Thu heaved a sigh: it was going to be one of *those* conversations. In truth, Bach Duong was now head over heels in love with Dao Que Chi. Dao Que Chi's beauty was so otherworldly that Bach Duong had already lost himself to the point of not daring to kiss another!

"Lady Thien, are you interested in young master Bach?" Xuan Thu asked wearily.

Thien Thien was stunned.

"How did you know I—?""

Xuan Thu said nothing further; she just gave Thien the I-have-known-for-a-long   time-but-didn't-bother-to-say-it look.

Thien Thien was silent for a bit, and then she declared: "I won't hide it anymore, since you already know. I am Princess Thien Binh!"

It was Xuan Thu's turn to be surprised, then. While at a glance she had guessed that Thien Thien was a girl, she would never have thought that Princess Thien Binh would disguise herself as a commoner.

"General Bach was very trusted by the emperor in the past. Bach Duong is talented, with unrivaled good looks. The Emperor will surely match young master Bach with me!" the princess admitted.

Xuan Thu's face fell. So that's how it was! Bach Duong was about to become a husband. His future wife had even disguised herself to keep an eye on him. It was a good thing he'd stopped flirting with everything that moved when "Thien Thien" had joined them, or else the trip would have been a complete disaster.

The two girls were still whispering together when a rattling sound came from the kitchen. Xuan Thu and Thien Binh shushed each other, ducking into the shadow of a garden statue to see what was going on.

Walking out of the kitchen came the Collector and the mutant, Big Bear.

"...Don't forget, the Poison Legion may attack and rescue him anytime!" the Collector said.

"Don't worry, my lord, with the Fire Beast and I here, anyone from the Poison Legion who dares enter won't make it out alive!" Big Bear growled in response.

"It is exactly because of the Fire Beast that I worry," the Collector continued. Big Bear closed the kitchen door, and the two men disappeared.

Thien Binh nudged Xuan Thu. "That part of the house is not really a kitchen. I'm going in to take a look."

"No! It's dangerous!" Xuan Thu stopped her. They should at least get someone else to come along. Bach Duong, for instance.

But Princess Thien Binh, who feared nothing between heaven and earth, ran into the kitchen despite Xuan Thu's objection. Xuan Thu couldn't stop her in time and had no choice but to follow; the two girls pushed the door open and peered into the darkness. The moonlight outside shone dimly, offering them no real light to see by, and Xuan Thu and Thien Binh were stumbling about, still not used to the dark, when a bright light came on behind them. Startled, they both turned around.

Fortunately, it was Dianthus, not the people of the Collector's Hall.

"This is where that evil Ngu Long is kept!" Dianthus held a lamp in one hand and a sword in the other, rage and hatred still etched into her face. She had searched too far and for too long to let the monster who had taken her son from her escape her blade now.

"You shouldn't be in here. This will be a dangerous fight. Go!" Dianthus moved forward as Xuan Thu pulled Thien Binh back, but Thien Binh was eager to have some fun and follow along.

Dianthus moved deeper into the building until she found a stack of split logs and a pile of hay. She pushed the hay aside until she'd found a secret door, and all three felt their way into a dark, narrow passageway. The walls were made of dirt, and smelled like damp, musty earth; Dianthus walked slowly, ears pricked in anticipation. Xuan Thu and

Thien Binh followed behind closely, and the three of them eventually reached the end of the hallway where a padlocked door stood. Dianthus slashed the iron chain, breaking it, and the door opened.

Ngu Long looked up. He was locked inside an iron cage.

"Prepare to die!" Dianthus sprinted forward to hack through the chain that kept Ngu Long fastened to his cage. At that moment, a figure shot out of nowhere and knocked Dianthus and the two girls against the wall.

Thien Binh and Xuan Thu were knocked unconscious by the impact, but before they went under, they could hear their attacker's roar: "Dao Que Chi, is that you?!"

Dianthus pulled herself back up and swung her sword just as the old man puffed out his chest and opened his mouth, sending out a blast of air that knocked Dianthus against the wall and sent her to the ground, too.

By the time Dianthus awoke, Thien Binh and Xuan Thu lay in a metal cage next to Ngu Long, unconscious. Dianthus herself was locked in the opposite cage. A strange, silver-haired old man standing outside the cage called out to her.

"Que Chi, answer me! Don't feign unconsciousness! I know you're awake!"

Dianthus stayed silent, still pretending to be unconscious. The mysterious old man persisted, still calling out the name Que Chi.

This continued until Big Bear stepped in. "Come on, it's time! We'll deal with this bunch tomorrow!"

Only then did the silver-haired old man reluctantly follow Big Bear out.

Dianthus sat up and looked around. The metal cage was solid; there seemed to be no way to break it. She tried knocking on the ground, the walls, listening for echoes; and after a long time she finally found what she was looking for: a weak spot. Just a gentle bit of force could break it little by little.

Outside, no one even knew the three were gone.

The second day of the event began without them. The people of the world would be presented with the holder of the Storm Pearl and the nymph, Dao Que Chi. Bach Duong had gotten dressed early, with the help of his seven women. Everyone assumed that Xuan Thu and Thien Thien would eventually show up in the evening.

The afternoon sun shone and the festivities began. Once again, there were performances of martial arts and music. Vendors at the Hall took the opportunity to sell roasted peanuts and paper fans to guests. By night, they sold umbrellas. The guest did not understand why; the stage had a dome. It was dark, but it wasn't raining. Just what did they need to shelter themselves from? The staff of the Collector's Hall offered no explanation besides, "There will come a time! You'll regret it if you don't buy one! Buy it! Buy it!"

The guests still didn't understand, but they saw that the umbrellas had "The Collector's Hall" written on them and bought them as souvenirs. After the umbrellas had been sold, the main event began. The Collector gave another lengthy speech, which was nothing but another advertisement for himself and how great his mansion was. Finally he gestured for Big Bear, waiting in the wings, to pull the curtain. Big Bear was about to bring Dao Que Chi out when the silver-haired old man walked out before the audience from the other side of the stage.

The alleged wanderer with the Storm Pearl should have been reserved for the final event. The Collector blinked in confusion, but quickly caught on.

"Introducing the ultimate hero, the new member of the Collector's Hall, who can take credit for capturing the villain of the Valley of Life and Death: the great Fire Beast! He is a force to be reckoned with, one who has honed his skills with the Storm Pearl in his body!"

So the man said to have the Storm Pearl had been recruited, and not caught!

Big Bear clapped his hands as a signal from the side. The Hall staff on the stage clapped their hands in response. The Fire Beast bowed his head. The man was old, in his fifties, with hair as disheveled as if he had just stepped out of a hurricane. His silvery-white eyebrows were straight as a ruler. His nose was hooked and his bloodshot eyes sparkled with fire, but also with the crazed gleam of someone who had begun to come unhinged.

Not waiting for the Collector's signal to start, he immediately launched into a display of power. From his seat, Bach Duong could feel a powerful aura from all four sides. The teacups on the tables clattered, rattling as they collided with each other. The tea in the cups shot up, stopped midair, and then was swept up in the wind and moved in a spiral. The Fire Beast roared and spread his arms wide, and this time the lights in the hall flared, sending sparks flying into the air. Fire and water merged in a beautiful, swirling vortex.

The Fire Beast manipulated the whirlwind of fire and water and it rose higher, blending the elements together. He stomped his feet, releasing energy that made the whole stage wobble. Fire showered down on the spectators, the water splashes turning into rain, each drop boiling hot. The Fire Beast laughed and his head shook, drool trailing down his shirt. The people who hadn't purchased an umbrella earlier cursed their lack of foresight.

The Collector, Quach Tam Phuong, was a bit bewildered by the Fire Beast's power display, but promptly announced to the crowd, "You have just borne witness to the Storm Power technique. One must swallow the Storm Pearl in order to master this. Except for the couple who invented the technique three centuries ago, the Queen of the Sun and the King of the Moon, until now, no one other than the great

Fire Beast has been able to harness it successfully. This is a legendary, unrivaled art form. The Fire Beast here is without a doubt the greatest of martial artists, and fortunately, from now on he will join the army of the Collector's Hall and stand by my side to hunt down outlaws in the Whispered World."

"Wait!"

This time Bach Duong stood up and interrupted: he was upset that his new outfit had been blasted by the blistering rain.

"The move that he demonstrated is incredibly powerful, but according to legend, the Storm Power involves controlling energy from the body. Although this person has immense power, this type of energy is not characteristic of the Storm Power technique! I have witnessed it with my own eyes! It was Obsidian, a King of the Poison Legion. The demonic Poison King was surrounded by black snow when he was around people, and when he attacked with blasts of wind, the snow would fill the air like a storm. The power of the attack comes from inside out, not the other way around."

The whole audience gasped.

"Does the Poison King have the Storm Pearl?"

"In the past, I heard that wherever Obsidian went, black snow fell, but no one knew why. Is it because of the Storm Power?"

"If the Legion possesses the Storm Pearl, and the Valley of Life and Death has Ngu Long, who knows the Storm Strike, and the Poison King has mastered Storm Power himself, why then have they not attacked and exerted dominance over the Whispered World?"

"What young master Bach said makes sense!" One person stood up. His name was Tu Thu, and he specialized in martial arts research. "According to my assessment, the technique of the Fire Beast is a variant of Lunisolar Power! It is close, but it's not the Storm Power."

The room fell silent, and Tu Thu explained further.

"Three hundred years ago the Whispered World was ruled by a powerful couple. They called themselves Sol and Lune, but to those of the Whispered World, they were known as the Queen of the Sun and the King of the Moon. They mastered the ultimate methods of martial arts and compiled their knowledge into a book called The Lunisolar Scripture, an extremely powerful manual. Whoever could master these forms and teachings would become undefeatable! To safeguard the world from chaos, the Lunisolar masters combined their powers to make the Storm and Sunlight Pearls before they died. The Scriptures were torn to pieces and scattered all over. In order to master the moves in the Lunisolar Scripture, one must have both Pearls and the complete Scripture.

"Since the book's pages were torn apart, what we have been able to recover is sadly out of its proper order. No one has yet found a way to combine the techniques and to use the two Pearls to achieve the peak of mastery. Those who train in fragmented parts of the Lunisolar Scripture are often overwhelmed by the power, thus losing their minds. The Fire Beast here is an example: his power is immense, but his mind is not stable. He has clearly been training in some parts of the Lunisolar Scripture, and is already affected by the power!"

Tu Thu paused and began to ponder.

"As for the two Pearls, the Storm Pearl has strong demonic powers, while the Sunlight Pearl has raging heat powers. Whoever takes them in will have their own powers drained by the Pearls, not even leaving them alive! The full Storm Power cannot be practiced without the Pearl. If there is indeed someone alive who can wield the Storm Power to its fullest extent, I, Tu Thu, would like to know of them."

The spectators began to whisper. The Collector—embarrassed over mistaking this variation of the Lunisolar method for the Storm Power—hurriedly licked his lips and spoke.

"Please calm down, everyone. Instead of arguing whether the Fire Beast has demonstrated the Storm Power or the Lunisolar techniques, we can ask this person!" He waved his hand as a signal, and Big Bear dragged Dao Que Chi out onto the stage.

CHAPTER 13

Brothers

"Miss Dao!" Bach Duong shouted.

Once he saw Que Chi, the Fire Beast's eyes burned with a furious gleam.

"You! I'll kill you!" He lunged for her.

Big Bear pushed Que Chi to the side and braced himself for the Fire Beast. The Collector also tried to mitigate the situation: he took out a piece of candy and tossed it into the Fire Beast's mouth.

"Come on! Be good!"

The Fire Beast sat down obediently, his hands on his knees, and started eating the candy. Que Chi was forgotten— for the moment. The Collector cleared his throat and tried to compose himself. He snatched the chain from Big Bear's hands and dragged Que Chi to the middle of the stage.

"Ladies and gentlemen, this girl is—" The Collector stopped, blinking, as a flurry of small, dark flakes began to flutter past his face. "...Black snow?"

"It's him!" Dao Que Chi breathed.

With a resounding bang, Obsidian swooped down from the ceiling like an eagle. His silver mask showed no mercy, his black coat billowing out behind him. Snowflakes and broken ceiling tiles rained down around his body. Gia and Ivy jumped down after him: Gia landed like a thrusting spear, crossing his dual sai daggers in front of his chest just as his feet touched the ground; Ivy touched down gracefully. Her multicolored skirt created a beautiful prism in the air, and her fluid fall made her dress cling softly to her shapely legs. Smoke from the copper vase in her hand billowed out throughout the hall. Ivy tipped her head back and let out a peal of cold laughter.

"Toxic smoke! Watch out!"

The audience covered their faces, but it was too late: they dropped to the floor like dominos, choking on Ivy's smoke. Bach Duong and his seven ladies-in-waiting rushed for the antidote, and the other fighters in the group tried to use their chi to draw the poison out.

Obsidian grabbed Ivy's hand and covered the smoking vase.

"Enough! There's no need for that."

"But I like it," Ivy pouted.

Obsidian jerked his chin in a silent order for her to move, and the three of them went straight for Dao Que Chi. Big

Bear, The Collector, and Bach Duong all converged on the stage to protect Que Chi.

Gia attacked ruthlessly, his daggers shining brightly in his hands. He always aimed the sharpest middle tooth of the dagger directly at his opponents' fatal pressure points, and the quillons on either side of the blade were just as sharp. One thrust could tear through skin and pierce internal organs—and this time, his daggers had more parts. They had heavy metal cores with several metal rings and black poisonous bells.

Gia held the dagger handles tightly, his thumbs stuck to the middle blade of the weapons to maneuver them. Three from the Collector's army rushed him, and before they knew it, two of their blades were stuck in between the dagger's teeth. Gia used his other hand to turn the handle upside down and strike the attackers' hands, and the sound of bones breaking filled the air. The bells on the daggers jingled with the movements of the handle, spreading powdered poison over the attackers.

The third fighter panicked and tried to escape, but it was too late: Gia caught up to him, clamped the man's sword between his own daggers, and broke it in two. Then, just like a cat playing with a mouse, Gia smirked, gently touching his finger to his opponent's forehead.

The fighter's eyes rolled back and he collapsed, and the spot where Gia had touched him turned black, the inky mark spreading out across his forehead like a spiderweb.

Next to Gia, Ivy jumped on top of another warrior, grappling him with her lovely, ivory-skinned legs. Just like Obsidian, Gia and Ivy were completely toxic. They could kill instantly, but Ivy enjoyed toying with her opponents, wrapping her hand around the warrior's throat and watching with a snarling grin as the poison overcame him

Gia cornered the Collector, who backed steadily away in terror until he fell off the stage. Gia was about to kill him but, out of nowhere, Ivy was tossed his way. He spun around to catch her, but she quickly regained her footing and pushed Gia away.

"Big Bear! You rat!" she spat in anger.

Big Bear was known as one of the Collector's most exceptional warriors, both because of his incredible strength and bear-like body, and because of the fact that his skin had been especially thick since birth. Thanks to training in the Impenetrable Skin technique, he was almost immune to external injuries and poisons.

So while Big Bear was nothing special as a fighter, his physiology was extraordinary. Using his bare hands, he lifted Ivy up in the air and squeezed her tightly, causing her to scream in pain. Gia stabbed at Big Bear, but with just one bellowing breath from the deformed master, he was blown away. The sai were useless against his opponent's skin.

"This guy is mine!" Ivy cried out furiously. She might have been stuck in the mutant's grasp, but she refused to let Gia have the glory of defeating such a worthy opponent.

"Whatever!" Gia raised his eyebrows, turning around to look for another opponent.

Ivy began to fume in Big Bear's grip: each metal piece linked together on her dress contained poison that could be released as smoke at will. Big Bear began to growl as the fumes became thicker and thicker, seeping into his nose and making him cough, burning his throat and eyes until they watered. He didn't even feel Ivy escape, and looked up to see her standing before him, waving her fan of needles.

Ivy laughed triumphantly and moved her fan through the air in a rhythmic, hypnotizing pattern. Her dress began to release smoke again, and she danced around as if from a dream, graceful and fluid as a paintbrush spreading color across paper.

While Gia and Ivy were fighting whoever had the misfortune of getting in their way, Obsidian went straight for Dao Que Chi without a word. His cold face showed no emotion despite the chaos around them, and he took her hand, calmly leading her away while ignoring everything else. Que Chi went along cooperatively, and the two of them made their way across the stage unimpeded.

An arrow came flying right for them and Obsidian used his staff to block it. The arrow went flying up toward the ceiling and hit one of the large, confetti-filled flowers that had been placed up there for the exhibition. Flower petals of all colors exploded into the air, releasing a fragrant perfume, joined in their cascade by sparkling jewels that reflected the lights beautifully; the colorful stones bounced and rolled as they hit the ground.

Que Chi brightened in awed surprise as the petals and gems rained down, raising her hands to catch some of the petals. She glanced at Obsidian. Just as they did to her, beautiful flower petals fell onto his hair and shoulders, the sparkling jewels standing out on his black coat. Obsidian blinked and stopped in his tracks, but still held Que Chi's hand; there, in the middle of everything, Dao Que Chi turned to him and smiled a charming, lovely smile.

"This is so beautiful, don't you think? I can't even tell we're in the middle of a battle," she whispered as petals fell onto her cheeks.

At that moment Bach Duong, still close by, tossed his bow aside and brought his sword up to Obsidian's chest.

Obsidian didn't move. Bach Duong came closer and grabbed Que Chi's hand, but Obsidian didn't let her go, either, resulting in a short, mortifying tug-of-war that ended when one of the men pulled too hard and tore her dress at the shoulder. A hint of annoyance crossed her face as she pulled her hands free and stepped back.

Obsidian and Bach Duong eyed each other stiffly, the tip of the latter's sword still pointed straight at Obsidian. Bach Duong wouldn't let Obsidian take Que Chi—and Obsidian had *had* it with his brother. All he'd wanted was to help Que Chi get out of there as quickly as possible! He pulled out his staff, and the two brothers were set to fight when Dao Que Chi suddenly cried out in fear.

"Help!"

Que Chi jumped behind Obsidian in fear: the Fire Beast had finished his candy and fixed his sights on her once more, picking up two chairs to use as weapons.

Obsidian and Bach Duong pushed Que Chi back simultaneously.

Obsidian usually used a staff as a weapon—but that wasn't his true weapon of choice. His cold, dark eyes gleamed murderously as icy energy from his hands seeped into the staff, absorbing the air's moisture and crystallizing it into ice. The ice spiraled up the length of the staff, turning it into a sharp, ragged, frozen blade, and black snow fell more heavily around him.

The Fire Beast grunted, hurling both chairs at Bach Duong and Obsidian, and both of them sliced the chairs to pieces with their blades. The Fire Beast started to laugh maniacally, lifting up a decorative flag from nearby. The tip of the flag burst into flames as his fiery power suffused it, and he waved the burning flag as an attack.

Bach Duong began utilizing the skills he had learned from Grandma Pink, the eccentric old woman who'd taken him and trained him in the place of his brother. She had learned and trained in the martial arts for the exclusive purpose of researching and keeping her body healthy, not for combat, which meant that her style was more gentle and defensive than aggressive.

Bach Duong yielded to avoid the force of the burning flag and use the Fire Beast's technique against him, but the Fire Beast's moves were odd and erratic, showing no weaknesses to be exploited. Bach Duong's skills with the sword could only help him protect himself; he couldn't deliver a counterattack effectively.

Obsidian rarely showed his true skill, but where techniques were concerned, he'd learned from Samsara herself, the Legion's evil religious leader and commander whose deadly methods *were* intended to kill. Unlike Bach Duong, his style was more toughness than tenderness, offensive over defensive. Obsidian had *also* absorbed the Storm Pearl, which made him especially lethal.

The Fire Beast didn't like Obsidian. After three strikes at him with the flag he shouted, "I'm not going to fight you," and then turned his attention to Bach Duong. The Fire Beast pushed more power into the flag, flames engulfing its entire surface. Bach Duong's sword connected with the flag, but it was jolted back toward him, sending heart-stopping panic shooting through his veins.

But Obsidian immediately intercepted the rebounding blade with his own sword, cutting the flag and Bach Duong's sword in two so the weapon would not kill its owner.

Half of the flag fell clattering onto the floor, and the fire from the flag spread out on the carpet, blazing fiercely. Bach Duong was just about to throw the broken sword away when Obsidian caught it and switched the blade with his own.

"Thank you," Bach Duong uttered in surprise. Obsidian used his energy to turn what was left of Bach Duong's sword into another icy blade.

Two young men. Two frozen crystal blades.

"Do you know the Advancing Magenta Sword technique?" Obsidian whispered.

Bach Duong nodded. The Advancing Magenta Sword was one of the strange techniques of Lady Pink. It was used solely for offense, and didn't have any power or protective effect, so while Bach Duong had learned about it, he didn't fully understand what it was for.

"The Advancing Magenta Sword is part of the Hundred-Year Dual Sword form! Make your move. I will fight with you." He waited for Bach Duong to prepare himself and then called, "Go!"

Fire Beast grabbed three more flags to attack. Although Bach Duong was a little skeptical, he still used the technique to group three flags together with his sword. Obsidian leaped up, using his sword to break the three flags, showering debris everywhere.

Bach Duong immediately followed up: the technique involved two people working in tandem to double the strength of their attacks. The Fire Beast used the broken poles to push back against Obsidian's attack, but Obsidian pushed even harder. The Fire Beast pulled his head and chest back, curving away from the blade, and was only pierced lightly by the tip of the sword in the middle of his chest—but blood still spurted from the wound when Obsidian pulled his blade back out.

The Fire Beast roared in pain and anger.

His voice resounded with power, shattering the sword. The broken shards fell, scattering on the burning carpet, and Obsidian quickly drew on his power to recover his sword.

Bach Duong and Obsidian stood together again, even more confident. It turned out that combining the Advancing Magenta Sword with Obsidian's Reincarnating Sword made the Advancing Magenta Sword a lot more dangerous, and Bach Duong suddenly understood.

"It comes to mind that your leader, Samsara, and my master Lady Pink were training and pushing the boundaries of martial arts together..."

Just like every living thing in the world, the martial arts needed balance. Yin and Yang. Toughness and tenderness. Attack and defense. Thinking that she and Samsara would live together forever, when Grandma Pink had found an incredible martial arts manual, she named it Bach Nien Giai Lao, meaning "a hundred years of happiness." She'd divided the techniques in the manual into halves, so she and Samsara could complete each other until the end of time. Each person was only supposed to train for their part, so that when they came together, the techniques would blend into one seamless whole.

No one knew then that Samsara had had an agenda from the very beginning. She'd studied both parts herself, then betrayed Pink and left with the entire manual. That was why Obsidian knew all the techniques, while Bach Duong only knew one half from Grandma Pink, losing the balance and effectiveness.

"Technique 6, row 10, page 8 of the Advancing Magenta Sword!" Obsidian called.

Bach Duong was even more astounded. "If you know all of my techniques, why have you never fought me?"

Obsidian didn't want to answer, and simply said, "Let's go!"

Bach Duong and Obsidian fought on, one in white, the other in black. Both seemed to have the same height and build. And they seemed to understand each other even without speaking: while one attacked, the other defended. The Fire Beast was forced to give ground beneath the steady onslaught of the two brothers' combined forces.

Bach Duong was fighting well, but his thoughts began to drift. He was floored: the man he'd been hunting day and night was suddenly on his side. Obsidian, who had always fled rather than face him, turned out to know him best. Not to mention the fact that even though he had a sworn duty to kill Obsidian, something felt right and familiar when fighting by his side.

Bach Duong's mind suddenly flashed back to his childhood, to running around General Bach's mansion with his little brother, Bach Phong. His short moment of inattention cost him, revealing the weaknesses of the Hundred-Year Dual Sword form to their enemy; the Fire Beast attacked Bach Duong with a powerful palm strike, and he spat up blood as the strike sent shockwaves of force ripping mercilessly through his body. The man might have been deranged, but his power wasn't something Bach Duong could match. Only one *powerful* palm strike could hurt a martial arts expert that badly.

Obsidian had thought Bach Duong was going to be able to withstand the assault, but Bach Duong continued to cough and spit blood as he crumpled to the ground. Had he not been wearing the mask, Bach Duong would have seen Obsidian's face turn pale—as if he were the one in pain.

The Hundred-Year Dual Sword form was broken. Distracted by his concern for Bach Duong, Obsidian was also hit by a powerful palm strike from the Fire Beast, reopening his injury from the last battle. Blood began to stain the silver fabric of his mask and roll down the skin of his throat—but he was much stronger than Bach Duong. Reinjured but still standing, he was only pushed back a couple of steps, planting his sword in the ground to regain his strength. The Fire Beast charged aggressively, infuriated that Obsidian was still fighting.

The fire that burned the carpet grew higher and stronger. The power of the Fire Beast made the flames spark and fly into the air, and the water from the audience's teacups was pulled up into the air, just as it had been before.

"It's the Lunisolar Palm technique!" Que Chi shouted.

Obsidian threw down his sword and lowered his head, his hands curling into tight fists: the only way to combat the Lunisolar Palm was the Storm Strike Power.

The liquid flying through the air froze. Wind began to sweep through the hall, centered around the one who had summoned it, making Obsidian's black coat flap and billow. Black snowflakes swirled with the wind, forming a kind of thickening, unholy halo around Obsidian's body. And on the floor, the broken ice pieces of sword were crushed and rose up in the air. The wind grew stronger, twisting and wrapping around Obsidian's body, obscuring him as it filled with snowflakes and ice-white crystals of glittering frost.

The Lunisolar Palm and the full-fledged Storm Strike were of the same origin: both had come from the Lunisolar Scripture. Countless others had looked for different ways to put the missing pages of the manual together, and different page combinations created different variations. Several martial artists had trained in the Lunisolar Palm, and although they had possessed extraordinary power, they had lost their minds in the process and eventually killed themselves.

It was useless to be the best.

The similarity of their origins made the Lunisolar Palm and the Storm Strike techniques equally powerful, and for those watching from whatever safety they could find, it was impossible to tell who would win and who would lose. The face-off between the Fire Beast and Obsidian reached new levels of intensity as the two powers filled out the four directions, rocking the stage.

The ground shook as if they were in the middle of an earthquake, and Bach Duong stuck his own sword in the ground, one hand pulling Que Chi down against his body to shield her from the wind—and the winds grew stronger still. The two forces clashed like opposing poles on a magnet, rattling through the crowd and worsening Bach Duong's injuries. Blood continued to leak from his mouth, staining his lips and chin a deep red. Gia pinned his sai to the floor, ducking to avoid being swept away. Ivy was in a much better position, having defeated the giant Big Bear: she just hid behind his burly body.

Among those on the stage, only two stood still. The Fire Beast's face was twisted into a ferocious, almost feral snarl, his hair and beard standing on end and waving with the chi that flowed around him. Ashes blew all over the place, mixing in with the jet-black snow still raining down around the King of Poison and being sucked into the wind like an obsidian cyclone. Obsidian himself looked deadly, his mask hiding his every emotion—which were already a rarity.

As the two opponents fought each other, the people still in the hall realized that while the Fire Beast was using external power just as Tu Thu and Bach Duong had described, Obsidian used the dark, cold internal power that had been ascribed to one who had mastered the true Storm Strike.

The Fire Beast blasted power through his palm. Fire shot forth like comets, aimed right at Obsidian, leaving trails of thick, black smoke. Obsidian used his own power to block the blasts, and the fierce, fiery missiles suddenly exploded along an invisible wall. The blaze soon changed its shape, rolling into a round shape then contorting: thousands of ice crystals had wrapped themselves around the blaze. The fire melted the ice crystals, but the ice reformed rapidly, choking the flames and extinguishing the blaze.

The Fire Beast's entire body had turned a burning red, his strength failing. Likewise, snowflakes had begun to form on Obsidian's long eyelashes because of the way the Lunisolar Palm's power blended with the cold energy from the pearl. The injury on his neck was still bleeding, and with every spurt, the blood turned into snowflakes as it hit the arctic chill of the air and hung there.

But even so, neither man backed down. Their palm strikes passed through each other's bodies. The gloves on Obsidian's hands gradually turned to powder. The Fire Beast was getting worried; he knew that if he continued to use his energy for the palm strikes, he would eventually touch Obsidian's body and be poisoned, and Obsidian's power had destabilized the Fire Beast's own. It became volatile, making him dizzy, and he suddenly stopped, mumbled something, and ran away.

Obsidian sank to his knees, shaking and encrusted with glittering black snow.

Dao Que Chi immediately started for Obsidian. Bach Duong tried to hold her back by the sleeve, saying, "Don't go, Miss Dao! He'll poison you!"

Dao Que Chi kept walking, even as Bach Duong held onto her sleeve, and the frayed fabric tore—revealing part of a tattoo of a black spider on her back. Que Chi turned back, smiling at Bach Duong over that same shoulder, and then knelt down beside Obsidian to attend to him.

CHAPTER 14

Loved One

Dao Que Chi slipped medicine from her pocket and handed it to Obsidian to help stop the bleeding. Bach Duong watched from his place on the ground as she trailed her fingers over the skin of Obsidian's neck without hesitating, her gaze intent as she tried to assess the reopened arrow wound he'd left days before. Bach Duong sat in shock as Que Chi touched the other man so calmly, so easily, without a shred of worry about the danger it posed to everyone else; so casually that the only explanation was that she had done it before, and knew from experience that she was immune to the Poison King's lethal touch.

The touch made Obsidian stiffen, and once he'd taken the medicine, he brushed Dao Que Chi's hand away and moved to sit, placing some distance between the two so he could begin to pull himself together and heal. Bach Duong expected the rejection to upset Que Chi, but instead she merely smiled in gentle understanding.

"How is it possible for such a fragile beauty like Lady Dao to have the black spider tattooed on her back?" Bach Duong wondered to himself, stunned. "Why would Dao Que Chi and Obsidian...?"

Another member of the Poison Legion, Gia, landed right next to Dao Que Chi.

"Cassia! Are you okay?" he asked worriedly, and Dao Que Chi shook her head.

"I'm fine, but Obsidian was injured, and Ngu Long was locked somewhere in the secret chamber."

Realization hit Bach Duong hard and sudden.

Dao Que Chi was none other than Cassia of the Poison Legion. Together with Ngu Long the Sea Dragon, they were the two most important members of the entire Legion. The very woman who had made Bach Duong's heart melt with her ethereal beauty, her gentle bearing and her grace...

Bach Duong wet his lips with his tongue, catching the iron tang of his own blood, coupled with sweat and the tears that leaked from his eyes, shocked and bitter, at that jarring realization. He pressed his lips together in a grim line.

"Bach Duong!" a voice called. "Watch out!"

Lady Dianthus ran in, her hurried footsteps echoing around them. She had escaped the secret chamber and had come looking for Bach Duong to help her rescue Thien Thien and Xuan Thu. Now, seeing members of the Poison Legion, Dianthus attacked. Ivy fired needles back at the other woman with a snarl. Dianthus deflected the needles with her sword, but Ivy whirled around behind her, mercilessly and rapidly firing until twenty different needles buried themselves in Lady Dianthus' back.

"Be careful, Mother!" Bach Duong shouted to his stepmother, anxiety and adrenaline thrumming through his veins.

The word "mother" made Obsidian go still. He opened his eyes, released the chi he'd gathered to heal, and rushed in to stop Ivy; but Ivy was quick, and as he snatched her arm and pulled her in to keep her from continuing their fight, Ivy released a snake from her clothes. It burst forth and sank its fangs into Lady Dianthus' neck, and its venom spread through her system as Dianthus fought to keep the snake from coiling itself around her neck.

Obsidian dragged Ivy out of the way and slapped her across the face. Hard, fast, and furious, it was the first time he had struck her, and she glared angrily up at him as blood began to trickle out of the corner of her mouth, leaving a vivid red trail along her chin.

"Do not forget you are the North King of the Poison Legion! *I* am your family!" she yelled, her eyes burning in her vehemence. Dao Que Chi pulled Ivy away from Obsidian, quietly separating the two with a touch that was both gentle and insistent.

"Come, Ivy," she said, attempting to soothe the girl and diffuse the situation. "Let Obsidian take care of his own affairs. We should find Ngu Long." As Cassia motioned them out of the hall, those enchanting eyes flickered over Gia pointedly, and, unhappy as he was with the Poison King's display, he still followed Dao Que Chi without question. Ivy didn't follow as quickly: she took a moment to wipe the blood from her mouth with her thumb, still furious as her eyes followed Obsidian; only then did she turn on her heel and stalk out after Dao Que Chi and Gia.

They would settle the matter at Hoa Hon Palace.

Eventually Obsidian was left alone with the groans of the wounded and poisoned—and with Lady Dianthus. She had managed to fight the snake off, but the venom was steadily shutting her body down, leaving her weak, hardly able to move; she couldn't fight as Obsidian eased her down to the floor and administered the venom's antidote, no matter how badly she wanted to: this man was clearly a member of the Poison Legion.

His lack of malice as he began to heal her slowly turned her wariness into curiosity: she was the only one being treated, out of everyone around her, and despite her hatred of the Poison Legion for what they'd done to her son, they harbored no feelings at all toward her. No love, and no hate. Why would anyone from the notorious Poison Legion save her?

Ivy's words began to play in Dianthus' mind once more. *I am your family*...what did that mean? Could it be that this masked man was...?

Lady Dianthus studied the King of Poison as closely as she could. The mask left nothing visible save his eyes, not nearly enough for anyone else to recognize him...but there was something about them that plucked at old memories, something familiar that she couldn't quite place. She knew those eyes, she *knew* she knew those eyes, and yet...

The anger she'd carried with her since that day vanished like so much smoke.

"You are..." Lady Dianthus trailed off and reached for the mask, but he caught her wrist and shook his head. "Have we ever met?" she continued, still watching Obsidian with intent suspicion.

He didn't answer. It was too risky, knowing she might still be able to recognize his voice and realize her obvious suspicions were correct...but that didn't make it any easier. His hand trembled and he carefully shifted his grip until he held only her sleeve, hoping she didn't notice, but it couldn't be helped. He was remembering things from long ago...Lady Dianthus and Lien's faces had been obscured by time, but the knowledge that he was sitting directly beside his mother, the ache of knowing and the shame of lying to her, were obscured by nothing.

Obsidian could not bring himself to look at her.

Bach Duong could tell something had changed. There was an odd tension in the air between Lady Dianthus and the Poison King, and Obsidian's reluctance to engage was far too unlike him, all of it evident even as Bach Duong sat healing himself. Whatever was happening, the only thing he knew for certain was that ever since they'd fought alongside each other, something in his enemy called to him and plucked at old memories, stirring them all like silt. Perhaps it was the painful internal damage and blood loss addling his mind, but he couldn't stop thinking about much happier days spent with his younger brother. With Bach Phong.

Obsidian stood and turned away the moment he was through healing Lady Dianthus' wounds and ridding her body of the venom. She struggled to her feet, gathered her courage, and called after him.

"Phong!"

Obsidian thought nothing of the way he stopped and turned his head back toward Dianthus' voice, his brain too fogged with exhaustion to check himself.

"Huh?"

Both Dianthus and Bach Duong went still. Shock shot straight through Bach Duong like lightning crashing all around him, shattering the air even as realization shattered the lid he'd held on those memories and sent them all rushing over him like a wave. He could see everything: Bach Phong, his five-year-old brother, with his bright eyes, thick, long lashes, and smiling face...the way he'd turned his little head and called to Bach Duong.

"Brother! There is a strange sound in the lotus pond..."

The scene melted into the present, where Obsidian stood looking over his shoulder just the same way, thick, long lashes that had never changed framing those eyes—eyes that were sadder, and a bearing that was colder, but the same eyes nonetheless.

"What is it?" Obsidian pressed. His exhaustion showed in his voice, the same exhaustion that kept him from realizing what he'd just done.

"Your name is Phong?" Lady Dianthus asked, her voice choked, her throat tight with emotion. Only then did he catch his mistake, and cast about for what to do as tears spilled over Lady Dianthus' bony cheeks, the product of the hope that her years of weariness and despair might finally have reached their end.

"Could it be?" she breathed. "That you...you are still alive? Phong...my child..." She trailed off, but it had given him a moment to collect his wits and come up with a way out. His eyes narrowed, as if he were faking a smirk under his mask, and he drew in a long breath.

"No. It's not. My name is Phong, but I'm not Bach Phong."

"Then why do you know my son's name is Bach Phong?" Lady Dianthus pressed. She didn't believe him, couldn't: she knew in her bones she was right.

The longer the conversation went on, the guiltier Obsidian felt, and he knew it would only grow worse the longer he stayed; so instead of arguing further he turned away.

"You have mistaken me for someone else."

He left without another word, and neither Lady Dianthus nor Bach Duong were well enough to give chase. As Obsidian stepped through the door, he heard a high, mocking voice singing:

"The lonely person walking alone, snow tenderly falling from the body…"

The voice continued.

"…It is sad, but unfortunately, it is inevitable, because his own family cannot touch him."

Obsidian looked over to see Switch, every word uttered with a sarcastic sneer, happily adding her own flavor to her translation of the old poem just to make sure the verbal barbs dug in as deeply as possible.

And there, to the side, was Dong Tu. She had obviously been standing for some time, her eyes red and knowing.

Dong Tu, Switch, and Anole had arrived later, when the battle was nearly over. Switch and Anole had not chosen sides as they rushed into the fray, moving fluidly from enemy to enemy; they'd fought alongside Gia and Ivy against the Collector's Hall one moment, and the next turned to fight against the seven women Bach Duong had brought with him. Dong Tu was no exception: upon entry, she had come face-to-face with Duong Kien Minh and Vinh Phuc.

"You're alive?!" they'd screamed in unison. Blood had spattered their forms, unnaturally pale as Ivy's poison took hold, and veins had bulged along their necks and foreheads. Dong Tu had tried to run past, but Duong Kien Minh, believing he still had the upper hand, jumped to attack.

But Dong Tu wasn't the same little dojo girl from the Luu family anymore. She'd trained with the King of Poison himself, and it had shown as she grabbed a weapon from the ground and used it to block Duong Kien Minh's attack in a fluid motion that sent both Duong Kien Minh and Vinh Phuc reeling. They'd both stammered for a moment before they collected themselves and glared at her again.

"You—you colluded with heretics! Don't expect to keep your life when you return home!" One of them cried. Dong Tu had ignored them: she just hadn't had the time to care.

By the time Dong Tu had finally arrived at Collector's Hall, she had put together the pieces of what had happened. From Obsidian being grievously wounded at her own funeral, to Cassia Dao Que Chi and Ngu Long the Sea Dragon being captured by the Collector's Hall while bringing the medicine needed for Obsidian's wound, forcing the Poison Masters to come to their rescue...Dong Tu knew she'd played her own role in sparking the clashes.

And, despite hearing the name before, Dong Tu had still been surprised when she finally saw Cassia for the first time. Cassia of the Poison Legion, Dao Que Chi, was a great beauty, not some ordinary maid. Such a beautiful woman, standing at Obsidian's side...

Dong Tu had watched as he was pulled into a fierce battle with the Fire Beast, and had seen for herself the stress of being faced with his family and the pain it caused to deny them; it had left her aching for him. And right there, in that moment, as Obsidian exited the hall, he *knew* Dong Tu had seen it all.

It left him feeling raw and restless, bared before her in ways he would never have chosen, and he was glad his silver mask helped hide his face and whatever it might have betrayed to her.

Obsidian didn't respond to the promptings in Dong Tu's eyes or Switch's sarcastic poem. He simply walked straight ahead, without a word or a look at anyone else. He cut a somber figure as he walked away, and as he moved, black snow formed in the air around his body and fell to the earth in mournful swirls.

———

That night, when everything had settled down (for the moment, at least), Anole and Switch dragged Dong Tu up the hill behind the Collector's Hall and pointed into the darkness at Obsidian, sitting alone.

"Your lover is sad!"

"He's not my lover," Dong Tu denied in annoyance—even if a part of her wanted it to be true.

"So what is he, then? You fought a great battle against Ivy to win her dear Phong at all costs! If he's not your lover, then what is he?" Switch pressed, winking at Anole. They'd exaggerated the story on purpose—Ivy would have tried to kill Dong Tu whether she'd accepted the challenge or not, and they knew it—but then again, it wasn't a total lie, either.

Dong Tu had no interest in playing their game, not when she knew it would only encourage them to keep teasing her in the future...but the image Obsidian cut, sitting alone up on the hilltop, broke her heart. It would be far worse to let him isolate himself and wallow in his hurt than to endure Switch and Anole's childish teasing later on.

"Bach Duong and your mother are going to be okay," she said as she climbed up beside him, leaving Switch and Anole to their giggling. As she moved through the grass, moths and other small insects scattered into the air. The world opened up before her: delicate white daisies seemed to glow against the dark of night, the whole vista bathed in moonlight. The world seemed to shift on nights like this, when the bright, gentle light softened some edges while sharpening others, making the blue-tinged world glitter as the light glinted off the forming dewdrops.

"My mother?" Obsidian asked in surprise.

"Gia told me who you are," Dong Tu replied.

"...I see." He didn't press for more, instead looking up at the sky. The night was quiet, peaceful compared to the fighting earlier. The breeze washed over them both, bringing with it hints of rosemary and the freshness of crisp night air; and the various chirps and calls of creatures in the night wove in with the rush of the wind in the trees to form a wild, soothing music. It was the kind of scene that wrapped people in comfort and made it easy to open up, a softer and more intimate space in which to exist than daylight could ever create. But Obsidian still wore the mask, and Dong Tu was sure he wore it to help him form the invisible wall he locked himself behind.

"The world has two types of mask-wearing people," she began softly. "One hides an ugly face, and the other does not want anyone to see his *true* face. And you..."

Dong Tu trailed off, holding his gaze as she reached for the mask. Obsidian caught her hand and held it, refusing to take the mask off. They stared at each other, neither giving ground...as he looked into her eyes and saw the steady gentleness, the genuine care, he eased his grip and finally let her remove the mask.

"You wear a mask to avoid killing. You have a kind soul."

Dong Tu and Obsidian looked at each other, maskless, face to face...heart to heart.

"No, no..." He smiled, small and rueful, and turned away. "Sometimes I'm the second type, too, not wanting anyone to know my true face." Sadness flickered across his face and cooled the light in his eyes, and his voice softened. "...Or also the first type. Wanting to hide his disgusting face."

"How could you be disgusting?" she objected. "I've always thought you were the most handsome man I've ever met." Even as she looked at him, the moonlight reflected in his eyes and made them gleam, brightening that handsome face. In his sadness, the heaviness of his gaze could cut to the quick and draw sadness out of others like venom drawn from a wound, making it almost impossible to look him in the eye for long—but his gaze suddenly warmed.

"Beauty and ugliness are in the heart," he chuckled. "The eyes look, but the heart sees."

Dong Tu's cheeks grew hot as she realized what he must have heard in her words. And if that was what he'd heard, it would have been no different if she'd confessed her feelings and admitted that he gave her butterflies in her stomach and her heart skipped a beat whenever she looked at him. Had she just confessed first?

Still blushing, she turned away and began to occupy herself with picking the daisies within her reach.

She'd been the first to kiss *(it wasn't a kiss!)*, and she might even have been the first to confess!

Luckily, that wasn't what he meant.

"Because you have a good heart, you see good things," Obsidian began, his gaze drifting and his eyes going distant as his mind filled with things she couldn't see. "When I look in the mirror...I only see a killer with his hands stained with blood."

Whatever memories took him, Dong Tu knew it must have been a kind of living hell, to make a good man believe he was nothing more than a monster.

"You must be nearly invincible by now," she pointed out. "Neither Ivy nor Gia could challenge you and hope to win. Why don't you go? Why not leave the Poison Legion and return to the Bach Estate? Bach Duong and Lady Dianthus would be thrilled to have you home at last."

He shook his head.

"It's complicated. You wouldn't understand," he denied, and Dong Tu didn't respond. Perhaps she wouldn't understand, but she couldn't help feeling like their situations were similar. Neither of them could return home: he was trapped because of the Poison Legion, unable to regain his identity, and she...because of Vinh Phuc, she could never return to the dojo.

Both of their lives had been stolen.

"Is it because of the poison?" she pressed. He shrugged with his mouth, neither agreeing nor disagreeing, and Dong Tu didn't try again after that. Instead she allowed them both to fall into silence as they watched the night sky.

Clouds passed over the moon, obscuring its shape and muting the light; as the moonlit shadows of clouds moved across the earth, it made it all the more difficult to read Obsidian's handsome face. He was beautiful, and she wanted to know him so badly, to be allowed to know and *love* him...but the mysteries surrounding him were tangled, like an ever-changing web, and she could not make them out.

It was the second time they'd sat and watched the stars together, but this time was different from that night in Hoa Hon Palace. They had both been lighter then, but now they sat, each struggling beneath the weight of their own burdened hearts, the silence heavy between them.

"Maybe it's because I was born under a bad star." He broke the silence with his quiet musing. "Maybe that's why my life has been such a struggle."

When he'd been born, his parents had been surrounded by enemies on all sides. Without Lady Pink, he would have been killed the moment he was born, but then...he'd only been allowed five short peaceful years before he was taken from his family.

"Did you know that Ngu Long the Sea Dragon was powerful, a formidable fighter, in the past?" he went on.

Dong Tu shook her head: she'd heard the name, but she didn't know who the man was.

"He was the man who developed the fourth move I taught you with the Rings of Thorns," Obsidian explained, and then, quietly, he began to tell her his story. He told her of how the Apothecarist of the Valley of Life and Death and assassin of the Poison Legion, Ngu Long the Sea Dragon, had been the one to kidnap five-year-old Bach Phong...how he was brought back to the sect and made to practice with poisons day and night; how he was immersed in thousands of poisons, taking them, being injected with them, being bathed in them; and how he was trained to use those poisons in fights.

How he had fought the other children to survive.

Life in the Poison Legion had been harsh and cruel, and children had died in droves, but Bach Phong had survived. He learned faster and trained harder than all the other children, even ones who had come before him, driven to become the best and fueled by one burning need: to kill the man who had brought him to that evil cult. To kill Ngu Long the Sea Dragon.

"Every time Ngu Long entered the training room, there was only one thing that came to my mind," Obsidian told Dong Tu. "This man was the reason I had been separated from my family. This man was the reason I was tortured and in agony day and night. My hatred knew no bounds.

And one day, about three years after I was taken, I had my chance."

———

Ngu Long entered the training room, and, as usual, he began whipping the backs of the children one by one. The metal spikes of the whip bit into their skin, cutting and tearing as the skin split—until they stopped. Phong stood glaring up at Ngu Long, his hand aching but steady as it held the whip still.

"So...you want to rebel?" Ngu Long chuckled. His voice carried coldly, and predatory amusement curled his lips. It had been a long time since anyone had dared to challenge him, and there was no way that *boy* would be able to defeat him. Not when the child was half-naked and unarmed, standing against Ngu Long the Sea Dragon himself, with his infamous Rings of Thorns. But it would make for a lesson the children would not soon forget, least of all the child before him.

Those watching crowded around the pair. Fights to the death were a part of life for them, and none would move to intervene. Bach Phong could see Gia, Ivy, and Truong amongst the faces in the crowd, and even their leader, Samsara, stood watching as the other children backed out of the way.

Ngu Long lashed out with one of his rings, and Phong dodged; but Ngu Long was too good to be thrown by a dodge like that, and he moved with the deadly grace of a snake, striking out over and over without pause. Phong just kept dodging, but the rings caught his skin nonetheless, leaving gashes in his skin that dripped and oozed deep, sticky red. No one was surprised when the first half of the duel ended with Ngu Long the victor, Phong panting and sliced to ribbons before the older man.

Even into the second round he could do little more than dodge those lethal, hoop-sized rings and try not to be ripped apart as he waited for his opening; but finally, *finally* Ngu Long gave him his chance. Phong did not dodge as Ngu Long looped the rings down over his head and body, despite the fact that if he moved the wrong way even for a second, all Ngu Long had to do was jerk those rings apart and tear him in half. Phong threw his arms around Ngu Long and flipped the rings from his body to Ngu Long's, and by the time the man realized what had happened, it was too late. Bach Phong flipped away from him, grabbed both rings, and jerked—

And slashed neatly through both of Ngu Long's legs.

It happened so fast that before anyone could register what had happened, Ngu Long the Sea Dragon lay on the floor screaming out his agony while blood gushed from his severed arteries.

But Phong wasn't done.

He took the rings, let his rage and loathing take him over, and moved to make good on the promise he'd made himself: that he would not rest until Ngu Long the Sea Dragon had paid for what he'd done to him with his life.

"Stop him!" Samsara shouted over Ngu Long's screaming. The other children rushed to obey, but they were knocked back and knocked *out* as Phong allowed his focus to narrow to the only thing that was important to him at that moment: reaching Ngu Long.

———

"In the end, I took one hit from Samsara and was unconscious for days. It was the only thing that could stop me," Obsidian finished. He smiled, but the expression was small and mirthless. "When I woke up, I was beaten and starved for days."

Dong Tu shivered, watching him with wide eyes.

"I didn't know you were so...formidable," she said, but in reality it was more than that. It was frightening. She'd gotten so used to the gentleness he showed her that she forgot: he was still the North King of the Poison Legion. He was still just as dangerous as he had always been.

"It's nothing to be proud of," he denied. "In our clan, you must follow the orders of the clan, even to kill. Although..." he added with a sigh, "that was the one and only time I truly felt the drive to kill."

After the incident, Phong had been cut off from the antidote given to the children to help them survive their training. He'd injured a Poison Trainer, a crime punishable by death, which meant his punishment was not only to be cut off, but to be cut off and left for dead. Others didn't make it through the first few days, let alone the weeklong deprivation. But at the end of that week, when Phong's death was meant to be confirmed, instead they found him alive. He was barely there: the young boy was wracked with agony as it throbbed through his small body, paralyzed with the pain and the weakness the poisons still suffusing his system had wrought—barely able to breathe, let alone cry out in his misery—but nevertheless, Phong had clung to life with everything in him.

It was an impossible, powerful sight.

"You carry great potential, little one," Thanh Nhan had murmured to the boy, and looked up at the young woman beside her. "Cassia, you know what to do."

Cassia nodded.

CHAPTER 15

Sisters

Thanh Nhan the Immortal's personal assistant, Dao Que Chi, also known as Cassia, had entered Phong's room. He remembered flashes through his mental fog: Thanh Nhan murmuring about his potential, being brought from his prison cell. He remembered being struck by the beauty of the room he was placed in, decorated with flowers and grass. They'd told him he had potential, but as he lay there, motionless, he couldn't imagine what it all meant for his future.

For a week Bach Phong had been beaten and starved and deprived of their antidotes; he'd been poisoned from the inside out, his own body toxic to itself. Between the fragrant, colorful flowers and the dreamlike haze the ordeal had left behind, he'd thought he had died and gone to Heaven.

Cassia's entrance pulled him from his haze, and his eyes fixed on her. He could see the antidote in her hand, but she did not move to give it to him.

"You must choose," she told him. "Life, or death?"

Phong hesitated long enough for Cassia to begin advising him on what would happen if he did choose life, and finally, before the poison took him beyond what she would be able to save, he chose life. She gave him the antidote, and, once he took it, she turned him away from her. His back was tattered and whip-torn, his skin mottled with bruises, and the merciful numbness that had pervaded him for several days vanished the moment she touched him.

Dao Que Chi took a needle and ink and began the meticulous process of working the image of a spider into his already-wrecked skin. It burned, not just like the sharp stab of needles, but almost like fire too; and the scent of flowers began to mix with something that smelled strangely like burning meat...

"Phong." Cassia gathered his attention through the pain. "Here in the Poison Legion, either you obey the Master's orders, or you will be put to death. Having entered this place is considered leaving all your past behind."

The black spider on his back was not only a mark of the members of the Poison Legion, but also denoted rank in the hierarchy in the Valley of Life and Death. Having chosen life had placed upon him a grim destiny, and had he been able to see it before he'd made his choice...he would have chosen the path of death.

By the time Que Chi finished tattooing, the antidote had also had time to do its work, and Phong was able to move. Once finished, the tattoo was painless, but tears still ran down his cheeks: he understood that from then on, he must forever be faithful to the Poison Legion and the Valley of Life and Death. Just like the tattoo on his back, he was there for life.

———

"Even if I killed every person in the Poison Legion, I still could not leave the cult," Obsidian confessed quietly. It had been a long time, but he could still recall every detail as if it had only happened the day before. He and Dong Tu fell into silence once more; Dong Tu stripped the leaves and petals from every daisy within reach while lost in her thoughts, until all around her stood thin, bare stems.

If Phong had to spend the rest of his life in Poison Legion, then Dong Tu would never be able to be with him. Only Ivy or Que Chi could.

"Lady Dao is very beautiful," she blurted out.

"She is an easy person to get along with," he agreed. He didn't see the way Dong Tu's face fell at his answer. Cassia was a woman of otherworldly beauty, and she had been in the Valley of Life and Death since she was a child. The magical medicines she had been surrounded with had only made her even more beautiful. She was dignified, gentle, charming, and a member of Poison Legion. Dong Tu was sure she could not compete.

Ivy was also beautiful, and a powerfully skilled fighter. Thoughts of the exceptional women who were always at Obsidian's side left Dong Tu feeling...out of place. She was just an ordinary dojo girl. She was not an ethereal beauty. She wasn't an incredible martial artist, either, and neither was she a member of the Poison Legion.

It was unlikely that she would ever be able to truly be with him.

"You probably like Lady Dao," she muttered to herself as her thoughts came pouring out.

Obsidian laughed, surprised.

"Dao Que Chi is a good girl," he allowed. "But..."

But she was a Poison Maker. Every poison he'd had to train with had been mixed by Que Chi herself, and there had never been a moment when training with those poisons wasn't excruciating. Even the spider upon his back had been tattooed by her own hand, and every time he looked at her, he was forcibly reminded of the pain he'd been forced to endure.

Of the destiny Bach Phong hated so deeply.

"But—" He finally looked over at Dong Tu, saw the hopelessness in her eyes, and stopped. "But you are the cutest!" he said instead, grinning playfully as he patted her head. "If I weren't a member of the Poison Legion, if I could touch people, I would spend every day with you. We would take walks, and play, and I wouldn't be afraid to hold you close."

Dong Tu knew he was flattering her, but that didn't stop the hope that rose back up within her, and in her mind even the daisies around her seemed to suddenly burst back into vibrant, flowering life.

"Who says I would let you?" she teased, despite the way her stomach fluttered.

Obsidian's playful smile widened, and he took Dong Tu's hand. She jumped, blushing as the warmth of his hands registered, and suddenly she found herself imagining what it would be like if he did pull her into his arms.

"If..." he began, laughing, a studying gleam in his eye, "If I could neutralize the poison and leave the cult...would you run away with me?"

The air left Dong Tu's body, and her eyes flew open wide as her blush darkened: was he truly asking if she would be his?

"I'm kidding," he chuckled, but his smile faded into wistfulness, all of his playfulness vanishing. "It's impossible." Obsidian looked back up at Dong Tu, and his smile warmed again. "But if it were...I hope that you would have."

The trailing sentence made her heart leap again, but she had no good way to answer him, still not sure if he was truly serious. Dong Tu playfully pushed him away and brushed imaginary dirt off her shirt as she stood up. She wasn't bothered by his teasing: the sky was full of stars, and she could tell that Obsidian had put aside his burdens, at least for the moment. The conversation had brought them both peace, and for the moment she was satisfied. But who knew what the next days would bring? Perhaps there would come a day when she would find a way to truly save Bach Phong from the Poison Legion...a day when she could be his.

"Here, you can have this back." She laughed, handing him his mask. It was packed with daisies, and he laughed as he looked at it. A mask full of flowers! He wouldn't dare wear it, but he did stand, his eyes shining once more.

"Thank you, Dong Tu," he chuckled. "Goodnight."

He waved at her, and they set off toward their rooms. They knew that Switch and Anole were likely hiding, waiting to ambush them with teasing questions, and indeed, the moment Phong turned his back the pair slipped out of the shadows and followed him. Dong Tu hurriedly fled before they could find her, but not even they could dampen her spirits. After consoling Obsidian and being consoled by him, even playfully, she felt like skipping the whole way back. Her head and heart were light, and she knew her night would be full of beautiful dreams!

When she made it back, the yard was dark and unnaturally quiet. The night breeze hadn't died down, but no leaves rustled: a strange energy suffused the air and seemed to freeze them in place, still as a drawing no matter what the wind did. Her room was dark, but as she walked inside, she heard a sound that made her stop.

"Who's there?" she called warily.

A shrieking laugh shattered the air to her right, and a figure leapt from the darkness, grabbed her, and flew back out the door. She struggled as they flew, and back out in the moonlight she was able to get a look at her attacker. The man had a snow-white beard and wild, soulless eyes.

It was the Fire Beast.

"Don't be stubborn, Dao Que Chi!" he shouted.

"I am not Dao Que Chi!" she yelled back, but the Fire Beast did not release her, continuing across the yard. His levitation skills were like that of a still wind: wherever he flew, the air seemed to freeze solid beneath his feet for him to walk on. He dragged Dong Tu into the false kitchen and entered the secret chamber. Inside, Ngu Long the Sea Dragon, locked in one cage, and Xuan Thu and Princess Thien Binh, locked in the other, had been arguing since the day before.

From the time the Fire Beast entered the Collector's Hall, Quach Tam Phuong had reserved this chamber for the Fire Beast to practice martial arts. After the last battle with Obsidian, his chi had driven him mad, and in his wild panic he'd grabbed the first woman he saw to take to the chamber and interrogate. Dong Tu didn't even have time to be startled at seeing Xuan Thu there before the Fire Beast began grilling her.

"Dao Que Chi! Tell me! The Lunisolar Palm technique, why—I used it, and now I'm *burning!* Why! *Why?!*" he demanded harshly. Dong Tu shook her head, terrified.

"I'm not Dao Que Chi!"

"Don't lie to me! Don't think that I don't know! You are the woman from the Valley of Life and Death, Dao Que Chi! You, it was you who read the Lunisolar Palm's secret to me! It was you!"

"No! I am Dong Tu! Que Chi is the beautiful girl!" Dong Tu denied desperately. Fire Beast jerkily tilted his head to one side, eyes whipping back and forth as if listening to a voice coming from inside his mind. He left Dong Tu, turned, and grabbed the iron bars of Xuan Thu and Thien Binh's cage.

"Then you two! *You* two are Dao Que Chi! Tell me! Why! Why! *Why?!*"

"Why what?" Xuan Thu demanded in return. Thinking she was Dao Que Chi, the Fire Beast drew in a deep breath, and bared and gritted his teeth to gather his chi. He tore the door from the cage with his bare hands in a sharp squeal of twisting and snapping metal, and sparks flew from the hinges as metal ground against metal before breaking. The Fire Beast walked in, grabbed Xuan Thu, and dragged her out of the cage to a corner of the chamber.

"Why, why? Dao Que Chi! Tell me why!" He pulled a few pages of an old book out of his shirt and slammed them toward Xuan Thu's face. "Read! Read it again! Why did I train...I trained! But the burning keeps rising! My head is burning! Why, why, why!?" he screamed.

Spittle flew from his lips in his rabid state, and the angrier he became, the brighter the torches on the wall flared, flames licking up the wall like they wanted to catch the place on fire.

Xuan Thu frantically grabbed the papers and scanned them intently: they were old pages torn from some old martial arts manual, with interlaced drawings and symbols scattered everywhere. She glanced fearfully up at Dong Tu.

"Okay, okay...I am Dao Que Chi...let me read."

The Fire Beast calmed under the impression that he'd finally found Cassia, squatting down to watch Xuan Thu fervidly. The torches followed suit, shrinking back down enough to give off a soft light.

"For this, you have to use Yin and Yang energy...take a deep breath in, gather chi in nam mon point..." Xuan Thu was making it up as she went: she couldn't understand what was written on those pages, and she hoped her answer would buy them time.

While Xuan Thu pretended to study, Dong Tu grabbed Thien Binh's hand and searched the room and her brain for a way out; but the only way out was blocked by the Fire Beast, and she wanted to be able to escape with her sister, too.

"What does that mean...the Yin and Yang energy, huh? Huh?" Fire Beast asked, but nevertheless he sat down and began to eagerly gather his chi.

"Release me!" Ngu Long the Sea Dragon called out from the other cage. "Let me out, I will save you!"

"Don't!" Thien Binh cut in. "That man is evil! He is not trustworthy, do not release him!"

Dong Tu turned to study the other man, saw his legs, and immediately realized who he was. She ignored Thien Binh's objections, slipped over, and removed the pin holding the cage closed.

As soon as the door opened, Ngu Long gathered his chi and sent his palm energy shooting through Dong Tu.

It passed through her body and hit the wall behind her, sending chunks of rubble flying, but while she clutched at her stomach, she'd sustained no great injuries. Dong Tu would have to thank Switch later, for teaching her how to turn her inner energy into a void.

"Why, you—!" She was too angry to think of a good word, but the Sea Dragon wasn't sorry. He was indeed a true two-faced member of the Poison Legion. He picked up his chains and rolled them up, but as he moved to escape, Dong Tu grabbed a chain and jerked him back.

"Get away from me! Do you want to die?" he demanded, his eyes gleaming with cold, murderous fury.

"You promised that if we let you out, you would save everyone!" Thien Binh argued.

"You don't want to live anymore, do you, little girl?" Ngu Long had been forced to listen to Thien Binh talking all night long and wanted nothing more than to shut her mouth permanently. He moved to hit her, but Dong Tu blocked his hand.

"You will not touch her!"

Thien Binh took the opportunity to slide behind Dong Tu, nodding in agreement and looking haughtily down her nose at the short, legless monster.

"You brat, how dare you!" Ngu Long snapped. Disfigured he may have been, but that did not diminish his aggressiveness by a single degree, and he rolled his chains as he sneered up at Dong Tu. They were just two little brats... one chain whip would kill them instantly.

"You must keep your promise and help save Xuan Thu from the Fire Beast! Please, call Phong for help!" Dong Tu pleaded.

"Who are you, and how do you know the King of Poison?" Ngu Long growled, pulling back on the chain. Dong Tu didn't explain: she didn't know who Thien Binh was, or how she and Xuan Thu had suddenly ended up imprisoned in the chamber, but her sister was still stuck with the Fire Beast and had no martial prowess of her own.

"You should have asked Bach Duong for help!" Thien Binh said. "Do you know Bach Duong? He's such a dandy, but he is a highly skilled fighter and is very well-rounded!"

Dong Tu frowned as Thien Binh continued to speak. Bach Duong was still recovering from his injuries in the other room; Obsidian was the only one of them who could fight the Fire Beast and save Xuan Thu.

Upon hearing the name of the Poison King, Ngu Long the Sea Dragon had relaxed his stance, turned around, and jumped away—but he was no less aggressive in the face of that knowledge, because when Dong Tu once again pulled him back by the chain, he whipped around to attack her with it. Dong Tu dodged, but the iron chain blew past and struck the Fire Beast instead, tearing him from his hyper-focused studying.

He roared. The torches in their brackets seemed to roar as well, leaping up the walls and splitting across their surface, crawling and writhing along the walls like a fire dragon. The Fire Beast flung his arms out and fire exploded from his body to form thousands of blistering, fiery arms, and Ngu Long dragged Thien Binh in front of him like a shield.

"Protect the princess!" Thien Binh squealed as the flames licked at her, filling up the room.

And Dong Tu used the Capricious Heart attack to protect Thien Binh.

The fire passed through, hitting the Heart. Instead of burning, it was pulled into Dong Tu's body, and as it did it sucked the Fire Beast's energy along with it: the decades of diligent practice in Lunisolar Scripture were siphoned into her body, and the Fire Beast was left drained of all his power. Dong Tu's defense had reversed his chi and replaced his internal energy with her own.

With the Fire Beast shaken and weak, Dong Tu launched into Sting of a Thousand Poisons, quickly striking his pressure points; in the face of her onslaught he fled in confusion.

Once he was gone she collapsed, her body smoking: she, too, felt like she was burning from the inside out. And as she lay there, the energies tangled—and the poison lying dormant in her body was woken from its dormancy and once again flowed through her entire body.

The last thing Dong Tu saw as unconsciousness took her was Xuan Thu and Thien Binh rushing frantically over.

CHAPTER 16

Stranger

While watching Dong Tu, Ngu Long had realized that, for her to have been able to use the Sting of a Thousand Poisons attack, she had to be connected to some high-ranking personnel in the Poison Legion. So when he met Gia, Ivy, and Cassia outside, he reported exactly what had happened. The three of them rushed in to find Xuan Thu and Thien Binh helping Dong Tu out of the chamber.

"I could finish her off with one hit!" Ivy exclaimed in delight. Gia stopped her, clicking his tongue.

"She's going to die anyway," he pointed out. "...What a shame that Phong's unlikely love story is going to be cut so short."

Some kind of emotion flickered across Dao Que Chi's face at Gia's words, but it passed too quickly to be read. She watched as Gia scooped Dong Tu into his arms.

"Little girl, oh, little girl," he whispered softly to Dong Tu. "You could have loved anyone else, but it had to be Phong. I knew this day would come."

———

Obsidian had chosen an empty suite to stay in that night, certain no one would visit him: they were all poisoned or injured in the main hall. The hallway had been deserted, every door shut, and the lanterns flickered as their weak light just barely held back the darkness. When Obsidian heard footsteps in the hall over the wind groaning outside, he stepped out to see who was coming.

He could see Gia carrying Dong Tu at the other end of the passage, flanked by Ivy and Cassia. Their dresses fluttered and flowed as they moved, Ivy in purple, Que Chi in white; they looked enchanting and ethereal, like fairies, but Obsidian's eyes were fixed on the motionless girl in Gia's arms.

A bell began to toll, the blood-chilling sound tearing the gloomy night apart.

Obsidian took Dong Tu from Gia and brought her into his room. He'd held her many times before, but this time... this time cut like a knife, sharp and aching. The wind still groaned in the darkness outside, the lights in the room waning; he gave her another dose of antidote, but the poison had taken over her whole body. There was nothing they could do.

Obsidian sat beside Dong Tu and held her hand, his eyes glittering with bitterness and anger. Dao Que Chi patted him lightly on the shoulder, but he pushed the comforting hand away. Across the room, Ivy watched it all with her arms crossed, teeth gritted in frustration. She thought about intervening, but Cassia caught her eye and shook her head, signaling for them all to step out.

"Leave Phong in peace for a while," she said, and sighed as she pulled the door closed behind her.

Xuan Thu and Thien Binh returned to Bach Duong, but he too shook his head.

"The poison on Obsidian's body has no known antidote anywhere in the world. My solution from last time can only be used once. If the poison has returned, nothing can be done," he said. He frowned in thought, hugging his chest, but the move tugged at his wound and sent a jolt of pain through him.

Obsidian watched over Dong Tu all night, his eyes fixed on her without blinking, and lost himself to the angry swirl of thoughts in his mind. He held her hand in his own: it was soft, but limp and motionless, and he could feel the way it had begun to cool. He brought her hand to his lips and brushed a gentle kiss to the back, and then pressed it to his cheek, letting the warmth of his own skin sink into her slender fingers.

She was just an average girl...yet when he was near her, she brought him warmth and happiness when no one else could. He couldn't reconnect with his family; he had no great soulmate beside him. There was no one to lift the burdens that weighed on his heart or chase away the coldness of the world around him. No one but her. No one but Dong Tu.

He couldn't let her die like that.

"I will save you," Obsidian whispered.

Almost as if she'd heard the words, Dong Tu shifted, her hand curling around to hold his fingers. He didn't move again for hours.

It was past noon the next day when he finally left his room. Gia, Ivy, Que Chi, Switch, and Anole were all waiting for him in the yard outside.

"How's your love?" Switch asked in concern.

"Dong Tu still hasn't woken. The poison has spread through her whole body." Obsidian shook his head. "She can't hold on much longer."

Switch glanced at Anole.

"He's admitted he's in love!" she announced excitedly. Obsidian didn't bother to correct her, but Ivy and Dao Que Chi both threw murderous looks at Switch.

"The only person who can save Dong Tu is Thanh Nhan," Obsidian mused. "I have to bring her to the Valley of Life and Death."

"Bringing her back to the Valley is no different than declaring her your lover," Ivy pointed out with a frown. "Even if you acknowledged it, Thanh Nhan won't save her just because of that. The poison on your body is the most lethal in the world; it's too difficult to make an antidote whenever anybody wants. And besides, we are not allowed to interact with outsiders! If you bring Dong Tu back, Thanh Nhan will most likely kill her!"

"I am not returning to the Valley as the King of Poison," Obsidian said, lowering his voice. "The Valley of Life and Death has always had a rule: anyone who agrees to drink the seven most fatal poisons of the cult will be able to request that Thanh Nhan save a life."

"Phong, are you sure you want to do this?" Gia couldn't believe his ears. "Not one person since the founding of the cult has drunk all seven poisons and lived to tell the tale. You may be a Poison Master, but Thanh Nhan makes no ordinary poisons! Even if you did survive, it could still leave you crippled or destroy your mind."

It was a terrible idea.

"Prepare the carriage," Obsidian ordered anyway. No one responded: the only sounds were the pebbles crunching beneath Ivy's feet as she walked away, taking her anger out on every step.

"Let me," Que Chi finally spoke up. Whatever Phong decided, she would support him. Even if it meant bringing the girl back to the hidden palace in the Valley of Life and Death.

———

As the carriage started rolling, Obsidian stripped off his usual black battle wear and put on an outfit befitting a commoner, made of light, poorly woven cotton. Que Chi, Ivy, and Gia each rode their own speedy horses. Switch and Anole followed separately, secretly.

They wanted to see how it all would end.

Obsidian carried Dong Tu day and night without rest, and in some rare instances, Dong Tu would wake to see him—exhausted, but carrying her determinedly. Whether they traveled by foot or by carriage, Obsidian kept Dong Tu in his arms, and as she slipped in and out of consciousness the only thing she could feel was him.

Dong Tu had been poisoned before, when she'd accidentally touched Obsidian the first time. As the poison had spread, weakening her, she'd been afraid she would die; but she clung to one goal, letting it become the only thing on her mind: *she had to get back to the dojo.* She'd thought about how to return to her family. How to prevent Vinh Phuc from harming the other people of the dojo. This time was no different, but alongside the smiling faces of the Luu family... her father and mother, her brothers...Xuan Thu, Bao Yen, Bao Thuong...there was someone else.

Obsidian.

The first time they'd met, she'd expected him to be an ugly, evil freak no one would want to come near. But behind the mask had been a shy young man, and as she'd gradually learned more about him, she'd found him to be remarkably complex.

He was outwardly cold, but warm-hearted. He was lonely, distanced from humanity...and in desperate need of affection. He wanted a soulmate. And although they belonged to two different worlds, there always seemed to be some invisible thread that connected them, binding them together.

She woke again, out of a dream where she'd seemed to be watching a stranger—and woke to find that "stranger" there beside her. Obsidian's presence brought her comfort despite her exhaustion, and she tipped her head over to rest on his shoulder. She was poisoned, and far from home, but his presence was still enough to bring a satisfied smile to her tired face.

The next time she woke, they were sailing down a river. On one side, the vast waters spread out before them; on the other, willows lined the banks, branches interlaced with branches. The sky was clear, and a cold wind caught falling leaves and sent them skimming over the surface of the waves. The willows' branches spilled mournfully over the water like the hair of weeping women, their long, thin limbs brushing against the roof of the boat and clinging to it while it sailed away, as if reluctant to let the ill-fated lovers go.

Dong Tu didn't know how much time had passed before Obsidian anchored the boat and carried her onto the shore. The river snaked between two soaring mountains that sloped down to the water on both sides, lapping steadily at the pebble-strewn shore; the shoreline itself backed up to rocky cliff faces on both sides, where centuries of flowing water had cut a canyon into the earth, and above them a precarious-looking wooden bridge stretched from one side to the other.

"Phong...where are we?"

"The Bridge of Breaking. We have reached the boundary of the Valley of Life and Death," he said stiffly. Obsidian didn't go directly to the cave, instead anchoring the boat on the opposite bank before he lifted Dong Tu once more and began his determined ascent up the stone steps that led to the bridge.

The Bridge of Breaking was the boundary between the outside world and the Valley of Life and Death. To the people of the Valley, the bridge was more symbolic than practical: they traveled in and out by the waterway below, and only outsiders would cross the bridge. Usually those who crossed it came for treatment, trading one life for another: two would enter, but only one would return. Those who crossed the bridge to cause trouble were not given the opportunity to return at all.

Crossing the bridge had a very different meaning for the children brought to the Valley of Life and Death. Walking across that bridge meant leaving everything behind. From then on, their whole lives belonged to, and depended on, the Valley. The outside world was dead to them.

From a distance, the Bridge of Breaking looked like an artist's brush stroke across the blue sky, but as he neared, Obsidian could see the planks and ropes of the familiar, unstable bridge swaying in the wind as it hung between one world and the next. When he reached the end, streaks dashed down the side of the mountain at him, one black and one red: two men landed and whipped their spears around to defend the entrance. Obsidian knew them as Ta Ve and Huu Ve of the Poison Legion, and while one wore a black robe with a red streak down its front, the other wore a red robe with a black streak.

Four other guards flew out to join them, but when they recognized Obsidian, they lowered their weapons and knelt down before him as one. He passed through the Gate of Ta Huu Ve and was met with two walls of guards in the same red and black: these were the ghost soldiers. They revolved upon detecting his presence to reveal still more guards of the Poison Legion, dressed in the black and red and motionless as the cliffs outside. Behind them the cult's flag fluttered, their spidery symbol emblazoned upon its surface. They, too, were startled to see the King of Poison dressed like an outsider, but raised their spears and knelt when they recognized him.

Behind the two tiers of guards were the people of the Valley of Life and Death themselves. Unlike the Poison Legion, they were dressed in white and bore no weapons. They drifted in loose clothes, wandering the yard like restless souls, and upon first entry they too met him with cold and emotionless expressions until they recognized him. But dressed as he was, they didn't know how to greet him: should they perform the customary greeting before the king, or welcome him coldly, like a pagan who had come with a request?

Obsidian didn't wait for them to make a decision. He carried Dong Tu deeper into the cave, ignoring the way their pale, soulless faces turned to watch them go. Their cold lifelessness was unnerving, and it raised the hair on the back of Dong Tu's neck, leaving her clinging to Obsidian's robe.

"It's okay," he soothed softly. "Don't be afraid."

Beyond the deathly outside, the Valley was like a fairy garden. Bamboo pavilions stood between lush herbal gardens, with immaculately manicured pebble paths winding between them, and everywhere flowers bloomed.

Their scent filled the air, fresh, pure, and lovely, like the garden of Heaven.

Dao Que Chi had returned to the Valley of Life and Death ahead of them. She came to welcome them and led Obsidian to his room to rest. His room was the same room she'd brought him to all those years ago, the same room in which she'd tattooed that spider upon his back. It had not changed, and was subtly similar to his room in Hoa Hon Palace: simple, spacious, with a collection of dried flowers and herbs. Obsidian laid Dong Tu down on the bed, but as he turned to leave, she grabbed him to keep him close.

"You can rest, I promise," he comforted her softly. "When you wake up, you will be as healthy as before."

"I can't," she argued stubbornly. "If I fall asleep I will die, and I will never see you again." She had changed between that first poisoning and the last: back then, she'd been certain she would die, and despite her desire to return to her family, she'd begun to give up. But not now. Now there were too many things left undone, too many things left unsaid, and the fear that lingered over everything else was the knowledge that she would have to leave Obsidian and the comfort of his embrace.

The strong aroma of the herbs in the room was lulling her to sleep, but she fought it desperately, terrified she would never wake again.

"On that day...on that day, did you really kiss me?" she asked.

Obsidian didn't answer.

"If I die without knowing the truth, I will die full of regrets," Dong Tu told him firmly. She could clearly see the wound in his neck from where she lay; after what the two of them had been through, there was no way they could just be friends.

"When you get well, I will tell you." Obsidian gave in with a soft smile, but Dong Tu frowned.

"How could I possibly get well?"

"Thanh Nhan will detoxify you."

"Thanh Nhan? Is she really just going to do it?"

"Yes."

"Are there no conditions?"

"No."

"There are *no* conditions?"

"None."

"Really. No conditions at all."

...Really no conditions at all.

Except for having to face seven different types of highly lethal poisons, but Dong Tu didn't need to know that.

Once Dong Tu had been comforted, Obsidian made his way to the Medicine Room to look for Thanh Nhan—and once again black snow drifted behind him, following his gloomy steps like a trail of ash. Dao Que Chi rushed out of the room before he could enter, holding a black robe.

"Phong, you cannot dress like an outsider, you'll anger Thanh Nhan!" she murmured insistently. She served by Thanh Nhan's side; she knew the other woman's moods better than anyone. "Wearing a cloth robe and bringing back a stranger is like telling her you want to leave the Valley. You may be asking for treatment, but it will still upset her." Que Chi studied him for a moment. "You should pretend like this is only business, a life debt, and not related to outsiders. You will have a better chance of getting her to agree to save Dong Tu."

She insisted again that he change his robes, and Obsidian reluctantly agreed, slipping out of his cloth robe. Cassia signaled, and two servants stepped out of the room and helped dress him in the black robe; she even carefully covered the bandage on his neck so that it would not remind Thanh Nhan of how angry she'd been when Obsidian had been shot.

Her caution was proven fruitless when Thanh Nhan's eyes zeroed in on his wound the moment Obsidian entered the room.

"Phong, how is your wound?"

Rather than answer her question, Obsidian instead laid out his request. The Medicine Room was empty as he spoke, and silent as the grave; it was so quiet that had the ash from the incense burning on the table fallen, the noise might have startled someone.

Thanh Nhan herself was silent for a long time, and when she spoke, she said only one thing. "I don't want to know who the girl is...but Obsidian, you have had too much drama going on lately!"

Her voice stretched every word in exasperation. The room remained still as she continued to weigh ingredients and medicines; even Dao Que Chi sat motionless beside her. Time always seemed to stop in that room, and nothing could urge Thanh Nhan to go any faster than she absolutely meant to go. The silence stretched uncomfortably before she finally broke it.

"Obsidian, you have begged, and I have no objection. But you know the law of the Valley. We have never simply saved people. If you test the seven poisons, I will heal the girl. No exceptions," she agreed, and Obsidian sighed with relief.

"I accept."

"Obsidian, I know your powers are profound. But my poisons are designed to kill people like you," she warned.

"Thanh Nhan, please. Treat her right away," he said firmly. The fact that he didn't waver rankled, but Thanh Nhan turned to Dao Que Chi nonetheless.

"All right. Cassia, prepare."

Dao Que Chi respectfully retreated, and Obsidian followed after her, rejoicing in his relief. Thanh Nhan watched them go with a thoughtful frown. The North King of the Poison Legion...he'd just been mortally wounded, and now he had brought a girl back to the palace.

Thanh Nhan both hated and loved Bach Phong. Hated, because he was the adopted son of Lady Pink: she had wanted to kidnap him and torture him to her heart's content. But loved, because the more he was tortured the stronger he grew. He'd risen to the highest ranks of the Poison Legion, just like she and Samsara had. Obsidian was their most devoted disciple, infinitely superior compared to the skills he would have developed under Lady Pink's training. But still, she hated that she'd had to snatch this success from Lady Pink's hands...

When Bach Phong was small, he'd depended on the cult. But he'd grown up, and his strength made even Thanh Nhan wary. He'd been born at the Bach estate, and he'd spent many years living with the Poison Legion serving the Valley of Life and Death...but who was he really? Would he be the next leader of their cult, dominating the world? Would he simply be one of those eighteen freaks wandering the world with no desire for fame or riches? Or perhaps he would be the son of General Bach, returning with his hatred to take his revenge. In her heart, Bach Phong was a son, a disciple, a successor—as well as a potentially deadly enemy. When the time came, what would he choose?

Should she kill him young, and eliminate the potential threat?

After all these years of being surprised by Phong, of being made so proud of the boy, killing him would break her heart. But if she didn't kill him, what then would she do?

Dao Que Chi wasn't gone long. She returned with the medicine for Dong Tu and the poisons for Obsidian: seven cups of poison for seven cups of antidote. She watched worriedly as Thanh Nhan picked up the powdered antidote and looked it over with disdain.

"Thanh Nhan, are you really going to detoxify Dong Tu?" Que Chi asked, and Thanh Nhan smirked, her face as wrinkled as a dried apple.

"If I don't treat her, then Obsidian's death will be in vain, won't it?"

"Are you really saying he won't survive? He truly is the greatest Poison Master in the world. But then, these are also great poisons..." Dao Que Chi was worried. She had no idea how all of this would turn out—whether he would live or die.

And then something struck her.

"You *want* to test your poisons against him, don't you. The greatest Poison Master against the greatest poisons."

Thanh Nhan didn't respond. Instead she slowly reached for her tea, and Que Chi quickly moved to pour it for her. The old woman took a drink and set the cup down; she

THE GIRL WHO KEPT WINTER

smirked at Dao Que Chi, showing off her toothless mouth, and beneath her heavy wrinkles there was a wicked glint in her eyes.

"This Dong Tu girl. Obsidian has endangered himself twice because of her," she said. "It seems I can't just cross my arms and watch forever."

Cassia finally understood Thanh Nhan's plan, but still it worried her.

And then she realized...if Obsidian had brought Dong Tu to the Valley of Life and Death, he must already have planned for it all.

———

The medicines and poisons had been prepared. Obsidian helped Dong Tu into the treatment room, the girl still unaware of the exchange that had been made.

"Thanh Nhan of the Valley of Life and Death has the antidotes to save other people?" she asked, surprised. "I've always thought this was a place of poisons."

"Medicines are poisons, and poisons are medicines. It depends on how you use them," Obsidian replied, his expression hard and impassive. Since his return to the Valley, he had become a completely different person: gone was his joy and relief at being able to save Dong Tu, replaced with a steadily building mountain of sorrow.

Dong Tu frowned, mistaking his sadness for anger.

"I'm sorry I'm causing you so much trouble, Phong," she apologized quietly. He looked up, realizing she'd misunderstood, and hurriedly shook his head, but before he could speak Dao Que Chi stepped out.

"Dong Tu, please come here." She gently pushed the bamboo curtain aside to let Dong Tu into the small room on the other side. Obsidian would be on the other side, both of them facing the curtain; that way he could be sure that after every cup of poison he took, Dong Tu would receive a cup of her antidote. Dao Que Chi saw the sickened look on Obsidian's face and stepped closer.

"Don't worry, Phong. Thanh Nhan's antidotes truly can cure any poison. When she steps out from behind that curtain, Dong Tu will be just as healthy as before."

"Yes..." Obsidian didn't doubt Thanh Nhan's antidotes, but...

"Dong Tu!" he called suddenly.

She stopped, having already ducked halfway into the other room, and turned around.

He took a step closer, took her face in his hands, and kissed her.

CHAPTER 17

Face to Face

Cassia didn't have time to turn away. Dong Tu was too surprised to react immediately: it was the second time Obsidian had kissed her, but for her, it was the very first time.

She'd thought about kissing Obsidian from the moment her lips had brushed his cheek, and it had only gotten worse as she developed feelings for him. She'd thought that kissing him would be sweet and gentle, but somehow, his touch felt bitter. Obsidian held her tightly against him, and his lips pressed hard and dry against hers. His stubble scratched at Dong Tu's lips.

Dong Tu pushed him away, her body reacting before her mind could catch up.

"Sorry." Obsidian let her go, but his hand lingered on Dong Tu's cheek, his warm fingers brushing her skin gently. His face showed no feeling. Even his eyes seemed empty, betraying only the barest hint of longing.

"Phong, what's going on?"

"Nothing," Obsidian answered, looking away and taking a deep breath.

Dao Que Chi bit her lip, her beautiful eyes troubled.

Obsidian studied Dong Tu one last time. One side of his mouth turned up in an odd little half-smile, and then he turned away, heading for the bamboo chamber on the other side of the curtain.

Dong Tu watched him go, troubled. That smile, and indeed, his whole demeanor, seemed strange. She would soon be cured; Obsidian should have been happy. He had carried her the long way to the Valley to save her, after all. Yet as he passed through the curtain and she sat down in her bamboo chamber, she couldn't help but think that his insistent, bittersweet kiss and the wry smile had all been a silent goodbye.

Dong Tu's head swarmed with questions as Cassia sat before her.

"There are a total of seven antidotes you will have to take," Dao Que Chi explained matter-of-factly. "The first antidote is from the extract of a hundred kinds of mushrooms. Miss Dong Tu, please take your time."

While in the opposite chamber, Ngu Long the Sea Dragon prepared to administer seven kinds of poisons to the very King of Poison.

The first dose set in front of Obsidian was the poison made from the extract of a hundred kinds of mushrooms, and he eyeballed the deadly cup on the table with disdain. As a child, testing poison in the Valley had always frightened him the most, before he'd finally grown used to it.

The first time he had been forced to test poison, Ngu Long the Sea Dragon had pinned him to the table by his shoulders. The toxin had seared his lips, bringing tears to his eyes. Choking, he'd struggled to escape, unable to speak or break free. Even now, he could still feel the memory of the pain that had set his every nerve on fire.

Yes, that boy had now become the King of Poison, but the seven poisons he was to face were unmatched. Compared to those, the ordinary poisons he had endured in his youth were nothing.

Obsidian didn't hesitate. He threw back the first poison coldly, without a blink, his face set. As the liquid slipped down his throat, he felt nothing at all.

The second dose was from the poison of a hundred kinds of herbs. He drained it all as well. His face remained the same, but when he set the cup down on the table, blood stained the edge of the cup, running down the side of the vessel: his lips were bleeding from the brew. But Obsidian had been doing this for too long. He barely noticed the sensation at all.

His stoicism pleased Thanh Nhan. Obsidian had indeed lived up to his reputation. Ordinary people would have fallen at the first dose, dying a quick yet agonizing death. At the second dose, only kung fu masters would be able to survive, and even they would have had to use their chi to save themselves.

For the King of Poison, the first two doses had gone down like water.

The third dose was a poison extracted from a hundred different insects. Obsidian's brow furrowed as he drank it, and he let out a heavy breath. The vast power of all three poisons was mingling inside him, truly beginning to absorb into his body and making it hard to breathe. Pain seared through him. He could feel the effects beginning to take hold, sapping his self-control. It felt just like the first time he'd tested poison, when he'd had no training at all. It left his body shaking, and the poison cup on the table seemed to be quivering as well.

Still, as Ngu Long brought out his sharp needles, each one dipped in a poison made from the venom of a hundred kinds of spiders, Obsidian rolled up his sleeves for the fourth dose no matter how hard his hands shook.

Each needle that sank into his skin left a blackened, diseased spot. As the poison ran along the bloodstream and sank into his body, veins of black spread under his skin, crawling across his hands like spiders. Obsidian ground his teeth. His body was fighting hard against the poison, and he could feel it all.

The fifth poison that the Sea Dragon dipped his needles into was from a hundred kinds of poisonous amphibians. This time, when the needles pierced his skin, even Obsidian felt the poison rush straight to his heart, clamping down on his lungs, trying to suffocate him. He panted, balling his hand into a fist and biting down hard, almost tearing through his own lip.

He reminded himself that for each poison he took into his body, Dong Tu would be given the parallel antidote. There were only two needles left. Dong Tu would be able to recover completely...if he could survive the last two poisons.

Obsidian raised his chi, adjusting the level of poison in his body, bringing Storm Power to his aid to counteract the poison. As the fiery toxin burned in him, the power of the cold was his best hope to fight it. As he raised his chi and its numbing cold swept through him, snowflakes arose around his body, each of them stained black by his contaminated skin. The more he dipped into the power, the thicker the black snowflakes swirled.

The sixth poison was made from a hundred kinds of snake venom. With the sixth dose, a pained grunt escaped him, and he slammed his fist hard into the floor. Sweat soaked his body, and his breath became even shallower.

The black snowflakes rose from his body in thick swathes, clouding the air like an icy fog. He'd known from the beginning that the danger Thanh Nhan had presented him with was not from each of the poisons individually. It was the combination of all seven kinds of poisons, taken one after another, combining their power to create the most unique and dangerous poison in the world—a deadly toxin that no one had ever conquered.

Thanh Nhan moved closer to Obsidian, raising his chin with a finger and studying his sweaty face closely. The black snowflakes that stuck to her skin settled into her deep wrinkles, darkening them like canyons carved of onyx.

"What now, Phong?" Thanh Nhan asked slowly; the sight of him seemed to pain her. "Perhaps you will not be able to withstand all seven of my poisons after all. It's not too late. You can still give up."

But this was the only time Obsidian had ever chosen to test his mettle against poisons of his own free will, and it was the only time he'd done so with true conviction. He forced his answer out between choked, labored breaths.

"Never. If—I give up now—Dong Tu won't make it."

"You're throwing away your life," Thanh Nhan replied resignedly, her voice heavy with regret. "But...suit yourself."

Thanh Nhan turned reluctantly around and nodded to Ngu Long: it was time for the seventh and final dose—the most lethal poison ever crafted by the apothecarists of the Valley of Life and Death.

On the other side of the curtain, Dong Tu had taken the antidotes from Dao Que Chi one by one. With each dose, the poison in her body weakened, the pain and aches leaving her. As she drank, black snowflakes began drifting quietly into the room. Dong Tu watched them and shivered at how thickly they swirled through the air.

The black snowflakes only grew in number with each dose of antidote she took; it seemed they doubled every time she drank, and the temperature in the room dropped more and more. By the time she put the sixth cup to her lips, the black snowflakes were falling into her cup and glittering darkly in her hair. They dusted Cassia's dress and patterned the empty cups on the table. They even formed a thin layer on the bamboo table.

Cassia dusted a snowflake off her dress and let out a soft sigh. Black snowflakes were not a good sign: the more Obsidian tapped into his chi—the weaker he became—the more snowflakes appeared.

Que Chi had watched as Obsidian was trained with the poisons since she was a youth. Although she was not a Poison Master herself, she had still felt the Legion children's pain as though it were her own; it broke her heart, knowing that the pain they'd experienced as children—that *Obsidian* had experienced as a child—was nothing compared to the agony he had to be experiencing on the other side of that curtain.

But the idea that twisted her heart most viciously was that while Obsidian was killing himself for Dong Tu, Dong

Tu had no idea what was happening on the other side of the bamboo curtain at all.

Cassia hesitated as she brought the last dose to Dong Tu.

"The seventh antidote is made from Ky Luong Di Thao, an amazing and rare ingredient," she explained, her face drawing tight with worry. The brew in the cup she held was dark and thick, and it gave off a strong, aromatic scent—strong, and extremely familiar.

"Ky Luong Di Thao? What is Ky Luong Di Thao?"

Dao Que Chi shrugged. "A type of ginseng."

It was by the talent of Thanh Nhan that some of the most unique poisons in the world had been created. And, in parallel to the virulent seventh poison, the antidote created from Ky Luong Di Thao was one of the most powerful the Valley of Life and Death had been able to cultivate. Without Ky Luong Di Thao, the Valley might never have been so feared and respected.

Dong Tu took the cup and breathed in its soothing, aromatic scent. The smell reminded her of thousands of regular herbs melded all together until she could not be sure which was which, but it was more than that. Somehow, the memory arose in Dong Tu's mind of the way she'd felt when Obsidian held her tight in his arms.

Just then, breathing in the scent of Ky Luong Di Thao, she felt a trace of that same warmth. It soothed her very soul, washing away all the troubles and leaving only comfort and peace behind. She drank, and as the medicine touched her tongue, its flavor flushed through her, rich and deep, like old, fine wine. It was the kind of flavor that was truly unforgettable.

Finishing the cup, Dong Tu could feel that the last traces of the poison inside her were finally gone completely. She felt the glow of health and vitality returning to her limbs. The medicine of the Valley of Life and Death truly was the stuff of miracles.

"Is Ky Luong Di Thao the kind of antidote that people of Poison Legion are allowed to use to detoxify?" Dong Tu pressed Que Chi. "Phong...he smelled just like this. Is it because he usually uses this antidote?"

Her heart stirred in realization.

"Is this the antidote that Phong had to rely on from the Poison Legion for his entire life? If...if one day, Phong had seven doses of this antidote, he wouldn't have to follow the orders of the Poison Legion anymore, would he. He would be able to leave the cult any time and be with anyone he wanted to."

The words Obsidian had said to her, that day on the hill behind the Collector's Hall, sprang to her mind: *If I could neutralize the poison and leave the cult...would you run away with me?*

Dong Tu breathed out. She spoke reverently, like one who had been lost and then, finally, saw a light amidst the darkness.

"How could I get seven doses of antidotes like this—to earn Phong's freedom?"

Cassia's voice turned cold and sharp.

"Do not call the King of Poison 'Phong' anymore."

She could no longer hold her tongue. She had to speak the painful truth. Like everyone around them *but* Dong Tu, she knew that Dong Tu and Obsidian belonged to different worlds. The ardor she heard in Dong Tu's voice was a childish fantasy. Cassia rarely spoke so bluntly; but, seeing the innocence of Dong Tu's hopes, she couldn't hold the cutting words back.

Her pretty face twisted with bitterness as she spat, "Because of your antidote, Obsidian has had to test the seven great poisons of Thanh Nhan! If you wanted to save the King of Poison, maybe *you* should have tried to survive seven of the deadliest poisons in the world."

At that moment, Ivy pushed through the curtain, her beaded chains tinkling. She strode right up to Dong Tu and shouted in her face.

"Do you realize what you've done?! No one has ever tested the seven poisons and lived. If anything happens to Phong, I will tear you limb from limb!"

"Wait," Dong Tu said, drawing back, "wasn't it you who withstood the seven poisons to beg Thanh Nhan to heal him?"

Only then did Ivy remember her lie, but she pressed on anyway.

"Of course not! None of the Poison Legion have ever completed Thanh Nhan's seven! They are the deadliest poisons on earth! Not one person who tried ever lived to tell the tale!"

Dong Tu's heart broke into a sprint, her chest tightening in panic. It couldn't be possible! Had Obsidian truly endured the trial of Thanh Nhan's seven most lethal poisons just for her? Could that have been why the King of Poison and Cassia had both looked so grim before he left the room? Had he left them forever?

Then it would indeed be life exchanged for life.

Tears welled in Dong Tu's eyes as she realized why there had been so many black snowflakes. The black snowflakes were generated by cold chi from Obsidian's body. And earlier, there had been an entire storm of them.

Dong Tu leapt up, running to yank open the curtain that separated the rooms. Her heart beat wildly in her chest, terrified at the thought that she would never see him again.

Please, please, don't let anything happen to Phong! Dong Tu repeated her entreaty again and again in her head. Obsidian had always treated her kindly—if anything happened to him because of her, she would regret it for the rest of her days.

But, just as she reached the curtain, Obsidian stepped out of the other room.

He was tugging a pair of gloves up over his wrists to hide the blackened, spidery veins the poison had left crawling across his skin. Seeing Dong Tu glowing with health again, the King of Poison's lips stretched into a tired, satisfied smile. He'd been hanging on for so long...since he was shot, he'd tried his best to continue on despite the fact that he'd never fully healed. With the danger to Dong Tu having passed, he was exhausted.

He was breathing, but his face had blanched to a sickly white; his dark eyes were dull and lifeless, the silver glint in them almost imperceptible. Yet there he stood: a peerless Poison Master, and the genuine and unparalleled King of Poison.

"You're alive!" Dong Tu cried, feeling like a great burden had lifted from her heart; the tears in her eyes shifted from sorrow to relief. Since she'd been poisoned, one person after another had had to suffer because of her—but the nightmare was surely over, and everything would be better. She rushed forward to embrace him.

But Obsidian stepped back, grabbing her hand and stopping her before she could reach him. Cold black gloves covered his hands, not leaving a scrap of warmth; for the first time, when Obsidian held Dong Tu's hand, his skin did not touch hers. His eyes bored into hers and his voice was flat.

"Dong Tu...you're free of the poison now. You cannot touch me anymore."

CHAPTER 18

Hearts Apart

Obsidian's chilling words left a bitter taste in Dong Tu's mouth. As bitter as the kiss they had shared before she entered the treatment room.

He leaned against the door, his fingers still gripping Dong Tu's through the glove. There was a glint of heavy emotion in his eyes, yet he seemed fulfilled. His voice was so calm and detached...as if he had been long prepared for this. And Dong Tu suddenly understood.

He'd predicted all of this. The moment he'd decided to bring Dong Tu to the Valley, he'd known they'd be torn apart. That was why, exhausted and tattered and yearning for the relief of sleep, he had insisted on keeping Dong Tu in his arms. He hadn't wanted to let her go, not even for a minute.

He'd wished for Dong Tu to be saved, even knowing the moment she was healed would be their last moment together.

Growing up in the Valley of Life and Death, Bach Phong had accepted his fate long ago. As the King of Poison he would never be able to do such an achingly simple thing as touching the ones he loved. He couldn't give any explanation to his brother Bach Duong, who pursued him year after year with the intention of ending his life. He couldn't acknowledge his mother, whom he had finally reunited with after so many years of separation.

Solitude was the only thing he'd known, and the only thing he'd expected, of his lifetime. All his old resentments were already buried deep. The child named Bach Phong had changed; his anger had been leashed, and the pent-up indignation in his heart had sunk deep below the surface, leaving only the King of Poison, cold and callous, hardened over from sorrow.

Then Dong Tu had come into his solitude, awakening parts of him that had been forgotten. He still remembered the moment when he'd bent to pick up his mask in that thatched hut and her lips had touched his cheek. When his hand had touched Dong Tu's skin in the middle of the forest, and his heart had filled with delight. But even then he'd known his moment of happiness would quickly fade.

There was no way he could leave the Poison Legion. That was an impossible dream. Even during his brief, happy moments with Dong Tu, he had been constantly aware it would not last. Every time they touched, he'd expected it to be the last. Every minute beside her had seemed to disappear like sand from an hourglass. Every time they'd reunited, he'd known they would eventually have to say farewell for good.

He'd known this when he kissed Dong Tu at her funeral. He'd known on the way back to the Valley of Life and Death, and he'd held her tight against his chest, clinging to that rare intimacy for just a bit longer. That beautiful night on the hill behind the Collector's Hall, when they'd held hands and warmed each other's hearts. Waking up under the sky by Hoa Hon Palace to the feeling of Dong Tu nestled in his embrace, silently wishing time would stop. Every single moment had been shadowed by the looming specter that was the *end*.

Through his long years of solitude, he'd never had anyone else. Only Dong Tu had been able to touch him like that, even so briefly. And it was time to let her go.

He gently squeezed Dong Tu's hand. The black gloves felt as heavy and cold as nothingness. The two of them belonged to different worlds: one was the King of Poison of the dark Poison Legion, the other only an average girl from a martial arts school. One's body was saturated with lethal toxins; the other would wither at the slightest touch. The one bond that had been forged when they'd accidentally kissed each other was now broken. Dong Tu had been detoxified. She could no longer be with Phong.

"You already knew..." Dong Tu was stupefied.

Obsidian forced a smile, gently released Dong Tu's hand, and slowly raised his mask, using the cold metal to obscure his face. He had already been prepared, yet he still felt the anguish tearing at his insides.

Dong Tu knew that would be the last time she saw the face of Phong, the man behind the mask. His dark eyes, with their long lashes and glint of silver, and the smile that brightened his entire face. From now on, she would only see this rigid and emotionless mask.

The person standing before her now was the North King of the Poison Legion.

"Then...when you kissed me before I went into the treatment room...that was goodbye," Dong Tu said softly.

Obsidian turned his face away from her. But Dong Tu took a step forward, reaching for him. Her nose burned and her throat tightened, yet her tears refused to fall, and when her hand touched Obsidian's once more, she felt the cold from it.

For a moment that could have been an eternity, they stood still, facing each other, grasping each other's hands tightly. The layer of the gloves separated them like a wall. They were so close, and yet that barrier between them was impenetrable.

Cassia touched Obsidian's shoulder gently, breaking their reverie.

"Phong, you're already tired. I have had your room prepared. Go inside and rest."

Obsidian nodded. He unthreaded his fingers from Dong Tu's, turning away once more.

"Wait…" Dong Tu cried, and as she did, her tears spilled over, streaming down and burning her lips.

Obsidian turned back around.

Dong Tu fell silent. Her eyes burned. Hot tears streaked her face.

"I…" Why was it so much effort to utter even a word? But she had to say something so that he wouldn't turn away. Not yet. Once he had walked inside, they would never meet again.

"Thank you," she said, and then burst into sobs.

It had come out all wrong. "Thank you" was pitifully inadequate compared to everything he had sacrificed. She'd wanted to say more, to try to find some way to see him again, but what else could they do? And what could she possibly say that could encompass all they'd shared in such a short time, and all that she'd finally come to realize she was losing?

That day on the hill by the Collector's Hall, if she had known they would never be able to touch each other again, she would've held his hand tighter and never let go. If she had known that bitter kiss would be their last, she wouldn't have pushed away in shock—she would have held onto his shoulders and never let him release her.

Obsidian didn't respond, but, briefly, a hint of that gentle warmth he'd saved just for her flickered in his eyes.

One last goodbye.

Ivy opened an inner door for him, and he finally turned and walked inside.

"And you go this way!" Ivy turned to Dong Tu, brusquely pointing her to the exit.

Dong Tu left the Valley with the two eccentric masters, forlorn. She walked quietly, tolerating their chatter and jokes and forcing herself not to look back. It wasn't until she had crossed the Bridge of Breaking, leaving the Valley of Life and Death behind, that Dong Tu couldn't help herself and turned for a last glance behind her, tears welling up in her eyes. The distant sight of the Valley beyond the bridge blurred with her tears.

"Farewell, Phong," Dong Tu murmured.

Switch and Anole glanced at each other in pity. How could they have led the way to such a heartbreaking separation between Dong Tu and Obsidian? They'd been expecting to be entertained by the dramatic turn of events, but Dong Tu's sadness overwhelmed even their careless, fun-loving nature. Dong Tu had been detoxified; it would be impossible to pair her and Obsidian from now on. The show had ended, but the two wanderers could not clap their hands in excitement.

The cold-hearted King of Poison had done such an outrageous, unheard-of thing, bringing a stranger into the

Valley and taking those seven extraordinary poisons to save her, only to be forced to separate from her forever in the end. It was almost the outcome Switch had wanted, but she did not feel fulfilled at all.

Obsidian and Dong Tu would never see each other again.

———

At last Dong Tu returned home, bidding farewell to Anole and Switch. As she entered the courtyard, weary and heartsore, she noticed the school was vacant. From the front garden to the back room, not a soul greeted her, only household furnishings sprawled in disarray.

On edge, she rushed out to the courtyard again, only to run right into a group of soldiers. They shouted at her, clapped her in chains, and promptly threw her in prison.

It was in prison that she was reunited with her family. Not until then did she learn that Vinh Phuc had known she was still alive when they'd met at the Collector's Hall. Upon his return, Vinh Phuc had brought a troop to the dojo and begun harassing the Luu family. His father, the magistrate, had charged the school with getting involved with an evil cult and conspiring against the royal court and had imprisoned them all.

Dong Tu's arrest completed his takeover. When he found out she'd been captured, Vinh Phuc strolled jubilantly into the prison to jeer at Dong Tu, intending to give her a last chance to choose to marry him or die. But as soon as he saw her tearful face, swollen eyes, and messy hair, he changed his mind and commanded that they be executed straight away.

Dong Tu barely noticed. Nothing seemed matter to her anymore: she spent her days curled up in misery, letting her tears fall freely. For the first few days in jail, the guards cruelly ridiculed and abused the whole family without end. And then, out of the blue, their guards became suspiciously polite and respectful.

Vinh Phuc's father himself arrived at the prison that day, but instead of further humiliating them all, he berated the guards for being disrespectful to the family—and even arranged for litters to carry them home. Dong Tu, shocked at the turn of events, had no explanation for the turnaround.

However, upon their return to the school, they found a roly-poly, odd-mannered fellow waiting for them.

Xuan Thu was overjoyed to see the fat man.

"Eunuch Trinh," she greeted him.

In the presence of the entire family, Eunuch Trinh solemnly read aloud a proclamation from the Emperor "rewarding Miss Luu Dong Tu and Miss Luu Xuan Thu, two heroic ladies who protected a royal family member so dutifully and loyally to the royal court."

From then on, under the proclamation, the magistrate would no longer dare to lay a finger on Dong Tu. Vinh

Phuc and his father were furious when they heard the proclamation's mandate, but they forced smiles, behaving as snidely as usual. They tried to gloss over their mistreatment of Dong Tu and the Luu family now that they were backed by the Emperor.

Dong Tu was grateful that her family had been spared, but she had no idea who the alleged royal family member that she had dutifully protected was. She couldn't make heads or tails of the situation, but she didn't inquire any further. The situation had been turned around and Vinh Phuc's family would no longer treat her family with cruelty; that was enough for her.

The rest of the Luu family seemed to take it for granted that the royal family member was the flamboyant Bach Duong, who had failed to kiss Xuan Thu.

Only Xuan Thu knew who the royal family member was. At the Emperor's proclamation, with a mischievous little smile, she said, "So that little eunuch knows how to be grateful, too!"

Xuan Thu would never reveal Thien Thien's identity, only putting on that same coy, mysterious smile every time someone demanded she tell them about the relationship between her family and the royal court. That kept the family and their neighbors guessing, and soon a rumor arose that the young master of the Bach family would soon ask for Miss Luu's hand in marriage.

The young master of the Bach family. Dong Tu always sighed at those words; there was another young master of the Bach family in her heart.

"It turns out that the two of them are real brothers," Xuan Thu said when they returned to their rooms, clicking her tongue. "Bach Duong lives happily at the general's estate, while Bach Phong wanders the world. The world is so wide, and yet, out of everyone, the two of them met and became enemies. What a cruel irony."

"The world is so wide..." Dong Tu pressed her face against her pillow and began to weep again. "When will I see Phong again?"

Xuan Thu patted Dong Tu's shoulder to comfort her, but her face showed no sadness, only an enigmatic excitement.

"You and Obsidian are not destined to be together. Even if you were to meet again, one of you would inevitably be wounded. You'll have to stay apart! Perhaps your fate is already sealed."

Dong Tu took this chance to cry even harder. "Then everything between Phong and I is over!"

Only then did Xuan Thu shrug her shoulders and smile mysteriously again.

"Not necessarily," she said, with an air that she'd been holding on to a great secret. "Remember the Stargazer's prophecy? That if you find a shard of the Sunlight Pearl for her, she will show you how to change your fate? Or that if you learn the martial technique of Sunlight Strike, you may meet the King of Poison again?"

"How can I find those two legendary treasures when even the top martial arts masters haven't been able to find them?" Dong Tu murmured, trying not to get her hopes up. She didn't quite believe in the oracle; it wasn't even clear if the Sunlight Strike technique and shards of the Sunlight Pearl truly existed or not.

"It's true, I'm not sure about the Sunlight Pearl." Xuan Thu's voice sounded thoughtful. Then, with a grin, she pulled some crumpled papers out from the closet. "But...you may not need it after all. Look at what I have here, sister."

She handed Dong Tu the papers she'd gotten from the Fire Beast—when he'd shoved them into her hands, mistaking her for Dao Que Chi, and forced her to explain what they were. Pages torn from the legendary Lunisolar Scripture itself.

And on one of the pages, densely filled with drawings and symbols, Dong Tu could see a technique entitled "Sunlight Strike."

(THE END)

"Xuan, ha, thu, dong, bon mua luan chuyen

Neu anh la tuyet, em se giu mua dong"

(Spring, summer, autumn, winter, the seasons come and go

If you were snow, I'd keep winter)

And so the story began, it was said that a girl fell in love with
snow and thus kept winter...

CREDITS

This book would not have been possible without the collaboration of a team of translators, writers, and editors.

Many thanks to...

...the daring team of translators, who tackled the job of transferring the strong culturally Asian style into English:

Phan Tu Tuan Cuong

Huong Chau

Nguyen P Ngoc Ha

Cam

Lara Nguyen

Chu Manh Toan

Thienthienngoc (I hope you bought the skates)

Dinh Van Tho

...the English writers and editorial team, who decoded the translation into an understandable and enjoyable read (and who were so patient that if aliens ever invade us, this group should be nominated as diplomats):

Ashley Sowers

Annie Phan

Phoenix Bunke

Chloë Womble

Fran Mills

Joni Chng

Kelly Ann Gonzales

Keith Richmond

Kim Fout

...the final editors, who adjusted the tones and style of the novel, restoring the beautiful language and keeping the spirit of the original text:

Ashley Sowers

Annie Phan

... ever supportive friends:

Mike Nam

Bien Pham

Ken Provencher

Dora Hsia

Sam Wen

Marlena Wong

Oanh Bui

Illustrator & cover designers:

Niayu

Rebeccacovers

Finally, thank you to all the Tuyet Den fans for your continued support over the past thirteen years. Without your encouragement, this English version wouldn't have been possible.